# INCIDENT AT MUSTANG PASS

When, on the death of their mother, Ben and Laura Johnson travel north into Montana to stay with their uncle, they little know what will be in store for them. First they witness a murder at Mustang Pass and then are involved in an ambush. What follows is an assassination attempt and an abduction. Added to this, they encounter ruthless men who are prepared to kill to get what they want. But, fortunately for the youngsters, they find a valuable ally in the famous Kentuckian gunfighter Jack Stone . . .

J. D. KINCAID

# INCIDENT AT MUSTANG PASS

*Complete and Unabridged*

## LINFORD
*Leicester*

First published in Great Britain in 2002 by
Robert Hale Limited
London

First Linford Edition
published 2004
by arrangement with
Robert Hale Limited
London

The moral right of the author has been asserted

British Library CIP Data

Kincaid, J. D.
    Incident at Mustang Pass.—Large print ed.—
Linford western library
    1. Large type books
    2. Western stories
    I. Title
    823.9'14 [F]

    ISBN 1–84395–168–1

Published by
F. A. Thorpe (Publishing)
Anstey, Leicestershire

Set by Words & Graphics Ltd.
Anstey, Leicestershire
Printed and bound in Great Britain by
T. J. International Ltd., Padstow, Cornwall

This book is printed on acid-free paper

# 1

It was the year of Our Lord 1879, and that late afternoon a warm September sun shone down out of a bright blue Montana sky upon the small cattle town of Mustang Pass.

There were few people in Main Street when the stagecoach rattled into town. As usual, however, a curious group of onlookers formed round the stage once it had been reined in outside Mustang Pass's inaptly named Grand Hotel. A two-storey, frame-built establishment, with peeling white paint and a general air of neglect, it was owned by Bartholomew Pickle, a reprobate who spent his days drinking what little profit he made. The Grand was the town's only hotel though and, consequently, any traveller requiring a room for the night was obliged to stay there. Such was the fate awaiting the seventeen-year-old twins who, that afternoon, climbed down from the stagecoach.

There could be no doubting that they were twins. Both were slim-built and dark-haired, with finely sculptured features and the same sapphire-blue eyes. The only discernible differences, apart from that of sex, were that Ben Johnson had noticeably shorter hair and was a couple of inches taller than his sister, Laura.

Both twins were similarly attired in check shirts, Levis, boots and brown leather vests and were wearing low-crowned black Stetsons. This was because, while the stage headed east from Mustang Pass to its destination at Lewistown, they aimed to travel forty miles northwards to another small cattle town, Boulder Creek in Miller County. And this final part of their journey must be accomplished on horseback.

At seventeen years old, Ben and Laura Johnson were orphans. Their father had died suddenly three years ago and their mother had taken his demise particularly badly. She had gone into a slow decline and followed her husband to the grave exactly two weeks earlier. Prior to this, however, she had made arrangements that, should she fail to recover from her malady, the twins would leave the family home in Springfield, Illinois, and go to stay with her bachelor brother and their only living relative, Henry Turpin, owner of the Big Canyon ranch up in Montana.

The driver handed down from the roof of the stagecoach the two small carpetbags containing the twins' scanty possessions. Ben took hold of both bags and turned to his sister.

'OK, sis,' he said tersely. 'From here on, we're on our own.'

'I know,' sighed Laura. 'You will take care of me, won't you?' she asked anxiously.

'Of course I will,' replied the boy, with an air of confidence he did not really feel.

The prospect of the forty-mile ride across the Montana prairie to Boulder Creek was not one that Ben contemplated with much relish. Although he and Laura could both ride, Montana was unknown territory to them and, so they had been informed, inhabited by Crow and Cheyenne Indians. Ben prayed that the Indians, should they encounter any of them, would prove to be friendly.

'What are we gonna do now?' enquired Laura.

'Wa'al,' said Ben, 'I guess we'd best book us a coupla rooms for the night, an' then I'll see about hirin' hosses to git us to Boulder Creek.'

'You don't think we should start out straight away?' said Laura.

'Nope. It'll be dark 'fore we can git half-way there. We could easily miss the trail.'

'I s'pose.'

'So, Laura, we'll git ourselves somethin' to eat an' then have an early night. That way, we can start out good an' fresh at daybreak.'

'OK, Ben.' Again Laura sighed. 'I do hope we're gonna like Uncle Henry,' she remarked wistfully.

'Sure we will!' said Ben.

Carrying a carpetbag in either hand, he led her into the gloomy lobby of the Grand Hotel. At the far end, Bartholomew Pickle's clerk, a whey-faced, balding man in a threadbare blue city-style suit, presided behind a large desk. He had Ben sign the register and took payment in advance. Then he showed the twins upstairs to their rooms. A man of few words, he informed them that dinner was at six o'clock sharp and, thereupon, promptly departed.

Ben stepped into his sister's room and looked around. It was sparsely furnished, with a cracked mirror on the wall above a small chest of drawers, upon which stood a chipped chinaware water-jug and bowl. He inspected the bed. At least it, like the one in his room, seemed to be provided with clean bedding. That, he concluded, was all that really mattered.

'I'm gonna see if I can find the town's livery stables an' hire them hosses,' he announced.

'I'll come with you,' said Laura.

'No, you stay here an' rest up. I'll be back 'fore it's time for dinner,' said Ben.

Laura nodded.

'OK.'

The boy smiled reassuringly at the girl and left the room. Laura sighed a third time, then took the room's single chair, placed it in front of the window and, sitting down, proceeded to stare out at the scene below. Not that there was much to see, for, now that the stage had departed, the crowd had dispersed and Main Street was once again pretty well deserted.

She and Ben were not the Grand Hotel's only guests, however. The room directly across the corridor from hers was occupied by Nathan B. Marston and a voluptuous young redhead named Kate Kelly.

Marston, large, fat and bald as a coot, was in town on business. But he liked to mix business with pleasure, and Kate Kelly was a sporting woman whom he had tumbled on several previous occasions. As the mayor of Boulder Creek in Miller County and a pillar of the community there, Marston had to exercise extreme caution when at home, particularly since he was courting a rich widow. Between them, they owned eighty per cent of the businesses in Boulder Creek, and Marston had no intention of losing her because of some minor indiscretion. Forty miles south at Mustang Pass, though, he felt perfectly safe to both indulge and satisfy his carnal desires.

The redhead, for her part, was only too happy to oblige, Nathan B. Marston being a generous client and none too demanding. This suited Kate, for the following evening, Saturday, the local cowboys were due to ride into town and she anticipated an exhausting though lucrative night.

Both she and Boulder Creek's mayor lay naked in bed, their bodies entwined. As their lovemaking reached its climax, Marston gasped with pleasure while Kate cried out in supposed ecstasy. Faking such a response was, of course, part and parcel of the sporting woman's art. Kate's had the desired effect.

'Pretty good, huh?' said Nathan B. Marston complacently, as he rolled off the redhead and snuggled up beside her.

'Wonderful!' she exclaimed. 'You sure are one helluva lover!'

'I bet you say that to all your clients,' replied Marston, with a grin.

'No, siree!' she lied. 'There ain't many can satisfy a gal like you can.'

'Wa'al, perhaps I'll pleasure you some more later.'

'Later?'

'Yeah. Guess a li'l rest is called for. Say we go to eat. That'll perk me up again; that's for sure.'

'You ain't aimin' to eat here, in the

hotel?' said the girl anxiously.

'Hell, no!' declared Marston. 'The food here stinks.'

'You can say that again.'

'I figure we'll mosey on over to Ma Jenkins' Eatin'-house. The grub's pretty darned good there.'

'OK. You wanna git dressed?'

'There ain't no particular hurry, honey. In a few minutes. Let's jest lie here an' cuddle some 'fore we go.'

'You're the boss.'

Nathan B. Marston smiled. He liked his women compliant.

While he and Kate were thus engaged, young Ben Johnson returned to the hotel. He went upstairs and tapped softly on the door of his sister's bedroom. Almost immediately, Laura pulled it open.

'You were pretty quick,' she commented.

'Yes. The livery stables are only 'bout fifty yards away from this hotel,' explained the boy.

'An' have you hired us a coupla

hosses?' she enquired.

'Sure have. They'll be ready for us tomorrow mornin', jest whenever we wanta start out,' said Ben.

'Good! So, what now?'

'Wa'al, dinner in the hotel is in one hour's time.'

'So, we eat. Then what?'

'It'll be kinda early, but I guess we'd best retire to our rooms an' try 'n' git ourselves some shut-eye. We've got a long ride ahead of us tomorrow.'

'I s'pose.' Laura did not feel in the least bit tired, yet she took her brother's point. Besides, she had no wish to traipse round this unfamiliar cattle town, certainly not in the dark. 'Come in,' she said. 'You can keep me company until it's time to go down to eat.'

'OK,' said Ben.

As it turned out, he and Laura descended the stairs to the ground floor only moments before Nathan B. Marston and Kate Kelly emerged from their room and made their way down to the lobby. Marston was now attired in a grey three-piece city-style suit, shiny black shoes and grey derby hat. His shirt was of the finest cambric. Kate, for her part, wore a low-cut, dark-red velvet gown, which displayed a generous portion of her ample bosom, and a dark-red hat to match. They left the hotel and headed across the street towards Ma Jenkins' Eating-house.

There they dined in some style, while Ben and Laura, being none the wiser, had to make do with the hotel's indifferent fare. The youngsters remained in the dining-room rather longer than most of the other guests, as neither felt particularly weary and did not want to retire for the night too early. Eventually, though, as the clock struck half-past seven, they rose and headed upstairs.

'OK, sis,' said Ben, when they reached Laura's bedroom, 'I guess we might as well turn in.'

'It's awful early!' commented Laura. 'I jest don't feel like sleepin' yet.'

'Nor me,' confessed her brother.

'Wa'al, come on in an' let's talk awhile.'

'OK.'

The twins entered the bedroom and, once Laura had lit the lamp and drawn the curtains, they sat down, Ben on the single chair and Laura on the edge of the bed. And they talked. The subject was the same one that had occupied their minds ever since their mother's death, namely their future. Would they like their Uncle Henry? What would life be like on the Big Canyon ranch? How would Boulder Creek, Montana, compare to Springfield, Illinois? These were only some of the questions discussed and debated. Then, presently, Ben pulled the gold hunter, bequeathed him by his late father, from the breast pocket of his leather vest.

'It's nine o'clock, sis,' he announced. 'I really do think it's time we turned in.'

'OK, Ben,' replied the girl. 'As you said earlier, we've got a pretty long ride to make tomorrow.'

'Good night, then, Laura.'

'Good night, Ben.'

Ben departed and Laura prepared for her night's sleep. But, although the bed was reasonably comfortable, she found that she could not drop off. She tossed and turned, then sat up and lit the lamp and tried to read the Bible her mother had given her, in the hope that that would send her to sleep. All to no avail.

It must have been well over an hour later that she heard the footsteps clumping up the stairs and along the corridor. They halted outside her door. Laura gasped and put down the Bible. She felt the hairs on her neck begin to rise. Some instinct deep inside her told her that danger threatened.

The sudden creaking sound of a door swinging open caused the girl to leap in alarm from her bed. Then she realized that the person outside in the corridor was pushing open, not her door, but the door opposite.

Laura crept nervously across the bedroom to her door, pressed her ear against it and listened intently.

She heard the door opposite continue to creak open and then suddenly, Nathan B. Marston's voice demanded:

'How dare you come bargin' in here? What the hell do you want?'

This question was followed by a pause and thereafter the same voice crying, 'No! For God's sake, don't . . . '

The sound of two shots terminated this sentence and were succeeded by a loud scream. Thereupon, a woman's voice added her shrieks to the cacophony, and a further two shots rang out, silencing her.

A terrified Laura had placed her hand upon the door handle as she stood listening. Now, startled by the gunfire, she inadvertently leant upon the handle and the door swung open a few inches. The scene she glimpsed horrified her. Laura quickly moved to push the door shut, but too late. The gunman, upon turning away from the scene of his crime, had glimpsed the door handle move and the door open slightly. He slammed the sole of his foot hard against the door and sent it crashing into Laura, as it swung violently inwards. The girl screamed and tottered backwards. She would have fallen had she not collided with the bed. As she steadied herself, Laura stared up at the tall, dark figure in the doorway.

The lamplight was sufficient for Laura to get a good look at the killer. He was a tall, rangy man, clad in a worn brown jacket, a white shirt with a badly frayed collar, a dark blue neckerchief, blue Levis and unspurred black boots. A low-crowned grey Stetson was pushed back to display a head of close-cropped black hair. Steely blue eyes glowered at her out of a harsh, hawklike visage.

The killer smiled coldly and raised his Remington revolver. Laura screamed a second time and threw herself across and over the bed, disappearing on the far side as the gunman fired. The bullet whistled an inch or so above her head and buried itself in the bedroom wall.

By this time the hotel corridor was no longer empty. Several guests had stepped out of their bedrooms, curious to see what was happening. Among them was young Ben Johnson. He observed the tall, dark stranger standing in the doorway of his sister's bedroom and immediately rushed to her aid. He hurled himself at the gunman, sending him reeling into the bedroom. The gunman lashed out as he stumbled and caught Ben a glancing blow with the barrel of the Remington.

Ben cried out and fell to the floor, but, as he did so, a couple of the other hotel guests appeared in the doorway of Laura's bedroom. The gunman hastily fired a shot in their direction, causing them to dive either side of the door. Then he turned and, stepping round the bed, confronted the trembling girl. Laura looked up in horror as the man raised the revolver, carefully aimed it at her head and squeezed the trigger.

The dull click told him that he had already had his six shots. He turned abruptly and then, realizing that his avenue of escape through the doorway was blocked, quickly stepped over the recumbent form of young Ben Johnson and strode across to the window. This he proceeded to throw open. Thereupon, grasping hold of the sill, he clambered out, lowered himself until he was hanging by his fingernails, and dropped to the ground.

By the time the first of the hotel guests burst into the room and reached the window, the killer had vanished into the night. Several others followed. They peered out of the window and stared anxiously along Main Street in both directions. The street lay in darkness punctuated here and there by shafts of yellow light spilling out from some saloon or store. But the gunman easily evaded these pockets of illumination and remained hidden from view.

While Laura attended to her brother and the guests in her bedroom continued to stare out into Main Street, the hotel proprietor, Bartholomew Pickle, and his porter arrived upon the scene. Pickle was none too sober as he stumbled up the stairs. However, the sight of the two corpses soon helped clear his head.

'Jesus Christ!' he exclaimed.

The porter, for his part, turned aside and promptly threw up.

Nathan B. Marston's naked body lay spread-eagled across the floor with two huge gaping bullet-holes in his chest and belly, a vast quantity of blood and guts oozing from the latter. It was the shot in the chest that had killed him, though, the bullet penetrating his heart.

Kate Kelly had fared no better. One of the killer's bullets had entered her left breast and the other had drilled a neat hole in the centre of her forehead.

Bartholomew Pickle and several of his guests were still gazing white-faced and shocked at the two corpses when Sheriff Jake Lucas clumped upstairs and pushed his way through the crowd into the bedroom. The sheriff was a big, square-built man. His rugged features contorted into a scowl as he viewed the bodies of Marston and the young redhead.

'Holy cow! Ain't that Nathan B. Marston?' he cried.

'It sure is, Sheriff,' replied Pickle.

'Wa'al, what in tarnation happened? Who shot him an' why?'

'Dunno why, Sheriff, but as for who done it, the shootist was a tall, lean feller who made his escape through the bedroom opposite,' said Ray Whitty, a whiskey salesman and the first of the hotel guests to have followed the killer into Laura's room.

'D'you recognize him?' demanded the sheriff.

'Hell, no! I didn't git more'n the merest glimpse of the feller,' replied the whiskey salesman.

'Anyone recognize him?' asked Lucas.

The others shook their heads.

'It's kinda dark out there in the corridor,' remarked Whitty. ''Sides, he had his back to us most of the time, though mebbe the gal across the way can tell you what he looked like.'

Sheriff Jake Lucas turned and peered over the heads of the crowd. He noticed the room opposite had its door open and the lamp lit.

'OK. Let's go find out,' he said.

He pushed his way back through the crowd and entered Laura's bedroom, closely followed by Bartholomew Pickle. Laura had by now recovered her composure, and her brother his senses. He sat on the bed and held a cold compress to his brow.

'Git them fellers outa here, Bart,' said the sheriff to Bartholomew Pickle, nodding in the direction of those few of the guests still peering out of the window. The hotelier did as he was bid and quickly shepherded the men out into the corridor. 'Now shut the goddam door,' barked Lucas.

Ben stared at the badge pinned to Jake Lucas's chest.

'You the law around here?' he enquired.

'That's me,' said the sheriff. 'An' jest who are you?'

'Ben Johnson,' replied the youth. 'Me an' my sister, we got off the stage a few hours back.'

'You plannin' to stay here in Mustang Pass?'

'Nope. We're headin' for Boulder Creek, up in Miller County. We got an uncle lives thereabouts.'

'Is that so? Wa'al, that's a coincidence, for the deceased gent across the corridor is, or rather was, the mayor of Boulder Creek.'

'Really?'

'Yeah. So, what can you tell me 'bout the shootin'?'

'Nothin' much. I heard shots an' came outa my room. Then I saw this dark figure standin' in my sister's doorway. He had a gun in his hand. I threw myself at him an' we both stumbled into the room. Before I could recover, he lashed out an' hit me with the barrel of his revolver. I guess I was temporarily stunned, for next thing I knew, Laura was kneelin' over me an' dabbin' my head with this here cold compress.'

'Is that right, miss?'

'Yes, it is, Sheriff,' confirmed Laura.

The sheriff turned his gaze upon the girl.

'An' what can you tell me 'bout the shootin'?' he asked.

Laura swallowed hard and then began. She slowly, succinctly, recounted all that she had heard and seen. When she had finished, Jake Lucas scratched his jaw thoughtfully and remarked:

'So, Miss Johnson, you got a good look at the killer?'

'Yes, Sheriff, I did.'

'Can you describe him to me?'

'Wa'al, he was tall an' kinda thin-faced, an' mean-lookin'.'

'An' what was he wearin'?'

'I . . . I didn't really pay that much attention. I think he was wearin' a brown jacket an' . . . an' a grey Stetson. It . . . it was his face I was lookin' at; his cold, steely blue eyes an' that icy stare that told me he was gonna kill me.'

'But he didn't kill you.'

'No; like I told you, he ran outa ammunition.'

'An' then he vamoosed through that there window?'

'Yes, Sheriff.'

'Wa'al, your description could fit any number of folks.'

'I'm sorry, Sheriff, it's the best I can do.'

'Would you recognize the killer if you saw him again?'

'Oh, yes; I sure would!'

'OK. I got me several 'wanted' posters in my office. Let's mosey on over there an' see if one of them matches Nathan B. Marston's killers.'

'You think the killer was mebbe an outlaw?' said Ben.

'I dunno. It's possible,' replied Lucas.

'You figure he was intendin' to rob Mr Marston? That that was what he was doin' here?' enquired the youth.

'Seems the most likely explanation,' stated the sheriff.

Ben Johnson nodded.

'Guess so. I s'pose he hoped to creep into Mr Marston's room, steal his money an' creep out again. Only that creakin' door wakened his victim?'

'Yeah. That's what I reckon happened.' Lucas turned to face Laura. 'If 'n' you'll git dressed an' step along, miss?' he said.

Laura glanced anxiously at her brother, who gave her a reassuring nod.

'OK,' she said. 'If you'll wait outside, please.'

Sheriff Jake Lucas smiled and left the room. A few minutes later, all three walked out of the hotel and headed towards the law office.

# 2

It was fairly late on the following morning when Ben and Laura Johnson finally rode out of Mustang Pass and took the trail north. Laura had spent some time looking through Sheriff Jake Lucas's wanted posters, but had recognized nobody. Both she and Ben had then found it impossible to sleep and, when eventually, they had dropped off, they had fallen into a deep slumber and slept much later than intended.

'D'you reckon we'll reach Boulder Creek 'fore it's dark?' enquired Laura, as they cantered along the trail.

'I hope so,' replied Ben. 'But we've got 'bout forty miles to cover. Therefore, it could be evenin' by the time we git there.'

'An' then we've gotta find Uncle Henry's ranch. He wrote that it was 'bout five miles outa town.'

'Yeah. Wa'al, once we reach Boulder Creek, we'll find someone to direct us.'

'Yeah.'

'For the present, we jest gotta keep followin' this trail.'

Laura nodded. She was glad that she had spent most of her childhood on horseback. Even so, she had never ridden through such wild, remote country and consequently she found the prospect quite daunting. She took some comfort from her brother's company, though she realized only too clearly the limited amount of protection the youth would be able to afford her. And, besides, she was still shaken following the events of the previous evening.

The first twenty miles proved remarkably free of incident. The two youngsters passed only two wagons and encountered but half a dozen travellers proceeding south; three cowboys, a Blackfeet Indian, his squaw, and a fur trapper.

It was as they began their twenty-first

mile since leaving Mustang Pass that they were overtaken by a lone horseman. He rode a bay gelding and was a big man clad in a knee-length buckskin jacket and denim pants. He wore a red kerchief round his neck, a grey shirt and a battered grey Stetson, and he carried a Frontier Model Colt in his holster and a Winchester in his saddleboot. Pale blue eyes looked out from a rugged, squarecut face.

The rider drew up alongside the twins, raised his Stetson to reveal a crop of thick brown hair flecked with grey, and said, 'Howdy, folks! You travellin' far?'

Laura glanced nervously at the tough-looking stranger, observing the man's broken nose and concluding that he was not someone it would be wise to cross. She was right. Since leaving Kentucky as a fourteen-year-old, he had, amongst other things, ridden herd on several cattle drives; fought for the Union in the Civil War; and, in the violent years that followed it, earned a fearsome reputation with the gun. Indeed, as the sheriff who tamed Mallory, the roughest, toughest town in all Colorado, he had become a legend. And that was when he had decided to settle for a quiet life. Not that it had quite worked out that way, for, although he tried hard to avoid trouble, it still seemed to find him.

'We're headin' for Boulder Creek, up in Miller County,' said Ben in response to the stranger's question.

'I'm travellin' that way myself. I'll ride along if 'n' that's OK?' said the man.

'Y . . . yes, fine!' replied Ben, although a little uncertainly.

'Wa'al, let me introduce myself. My name's Jack Stone,' said the stranger.

'Ben Johnson. An' this is my twin sister, Laura.'

'You're kinda young to be travellin' these parts jest the two of you.'

'Our parents are dead. We've left our home in Springfield, Illinois, an' are goin' to stay with our Uncle Henry. He owns the Big Canyon ranch outside Boulder Creek.'

The Kentuckian smiled sympathetically.

'I'm sorry 'bout your folks, an' I sure hope it works out for you,' he declared.

'Thanks, Mr Stone,' said Ben.

'An' where exactly are you headed?' enquired Laura.

'A li'l further north than you. Great Falls. I intend spendin' the winter there, helpin' out a coupla old friends. They run a hoss ranch, only Gus has gone an' broken his leg an' his wife, Frances, needs some help. I heard this news from a mutual friend, a cattle dealer, an' I wired 'em from Casper, Wyomin', to say I was comin'.'

'You must be pretty good friends if you're prepared to ride all that way to help out,' commented Ben.

'We are,' said the Kentuckian. 'Gus an' me, we served together in the Union army durin' the Civil War.'

'You were a soldier once?'

'Yeah; I been most things in my time:

soldier, peace officer . . . '

'You mean you were a sheriff, or a US marshal, or . . . ?'

'Both. But that's all behind me. These days, I'm lookin' for a li'l peace an' quiet. I don't figure on . . . '

But Stone never did say what he didn't figure on, for, at that moment, a shot rang out. Stone felt it whistle past his left ear and promptly reined in the gelding and leapt from the saddle. Leading the animal by its bridle, he dashed for the cover of a tumble of boulders. His two young companions were quick to follow. As all three hastily left the trail and dived behind this natural refuge, a volley of shots struck the rocks in front of them and ricocheted off in all directions.

'Goddamit! Road agents!' rasped Stone.

'Road agents?' enquired Ben.

'Bandits. Though why in tarnation they should've picked on us to rob beats me! We don't none of us look as if we'd be carryin' much cash.' Stone eyed the youngster speculatively. 'You use a rifle, son?' he asked.

'Yessir,' replied Ben eagerly.

'Good!' Stone reached up and pulled the Winchester from his saddleboot. He handed it to the youngster. Then, from one of his saddlebags, he produced a box of .44 calibre centre-fire cartridges. He gave this to Ben. 'I figure there's definitely more 'n one of 'em. An' they seem to be up on them bluffs on the far side of the trail. Reckon they got us pinned down,' he remarked.

'Guess so,' said Ben, as another volley of shots pinged off the boulders in front of them.

'Therefore, to git us outa this hole, I'm gonna have to work my way round yonder.' Stone indicated a bend in the trail where an overhand hid it from the view of their attackers. 'Once across the trail, I aim to creep up on 'em unobserved an' let 'em have it. But you're gonna need to cover me. Think you can do that, Ben?'

'Yessir, Mr Stone. You can rely on

me,' said the boy.

'OK, but keep your head down. An' that applies to you, too, miss,' Stone added, glancing at the white-faced Laura.

Laura nodded nervously.

'I . . . I will, Mr Stone,' she promised.

'Jest fire off a coupla shots every few seconds,' Stone instructed Ben. 'That should keep the varmints occupied, an' make 'em think we're all still pegged down amongst these here rocks.'

'You . . . you think so?' said Ben.

'It had better,' replied Stone grimly. He clapped the youth on the shoulder. 'OK start shootin',' he growled.

While Ben began firing in the direction of the bluffs opposite, Stone crawled on his belly towards the bend in the trail. This was situated about fifty yards ahead of the tumble of rocks, but fortunately a shallow arroyo ran alongside the trail. The big Kentuckian dropped down into this dry watercourse and, thereby remaining hidden from sight, continued his crawl towards the bend.

Dusty and sweating profusely, he eventually reached the bend and scrambled round it. When he reached the far side, the overhang shielded him from the gunmen on the bluffs. Behind him, young Ben Johnson was keeping up a steady fire in response to the bandits' bombardment of his and his sister's hiding-place.

Stone smiled grimly and, clambering to his feet, sprinted across the trail into the shadow of the overhang. Then, cautiously working his way round it and away from the scene of conflict, he found himself at the foot of a rock-strewn slope leading up to the top of the bluffs. Slowly, laboriously, Stone began the ascent. He picked his way between the boulders, his eyes peeled for any sight of the bandits.

They, for their part, were each crouching behind a rock and blasting away at the tumble of boulders where, they assumed, all three of their intended victims were cowering.

There were three of them, all wanted men with a price on their heads. Long Tom Nixon was a thin, lanky man with cold grey eyes, a long nose and a rat-trap of a mouth. Lank black hair hung shoulder-length from beneath his brown derby hat and his upper lip was embellished with a drooping moustache. His companions, Vince Brodie and Bobcat Deevers, on the other hand, were both short, stocky men. Tough-looking, mean-eyed characters, they were heavily bearded and could have been taken for brothers. They too were clad like Nixon in brown derbys and long, ankle-length brown leather coats. They each carried a Colt Peacemaker in their holsters, but were firing at Ben Johnson with rifles. Long Tom Nixon was using an ancient Colt Hartford, while the other two had Winchesters.

So intent were the outlaws on exchanging shots with the youngster that they failed to observe the Kentuckian as he silently dodged through the scattering of boulders and drew closer and closer to their vantage point.

Stone eventually crouched down behind a rock not twenty yards from the nearest of the three gunmen, Long Tom Nixon. He drew the Frontier Model Colt from its holster and carefully aimed it at Nixon. He squeezed the trigger. The slug struck the outlaw in the side of the head and blew his brains out.

As Long Tom Nixon hit the deck, his two companions leapt to their feet in shock. This was not the wisest of moves, for immediately they exposed themselves to Ben Johnson's gunfire and, unluckily for Vince Brodie, one of the youngster's shots hit him in the left shoulder and knocked him down. Bobcat Deevers, meantime, exchanged shots with the Kentuckian.

Caught off-balance and firing hurriedly, Deevers loosed off three wild shots, none of which came within two feet of the Kentuckian. Stone responded with a coolness born of many past gunfights. He calmly planted two slugs into the outlaw's body. The first struck him in the chest and the second in the belly. Bobcat Deevers sank to his knees, dropped his revolver and grasped at his belly in a desperate yet hopeless attempt to prevent his guts spilling out. Stone smiled coldly, stepped up close and despatched him with a third shot, this time between the eyes.

While Stone was exchanging shots with Bobcat Deevers, Vince Brodie was struggling to stanch the flow of blood from his shoulder wound. He made no attempt to raise the Colt Peacemaker in his right hand as Stone approached. He had had enough.

'OK,' he gasped, 'I surrender.'

'But I ain't takin' prisoners,' said Stone, and promptly shot the outlaw dead.

The Kentuckian held to a simple philosophy: namely that all outlaws were vermin, and the only thing to do with vermin was to shoot them.

He slowly made his way back down

to the trail and a few minutes later rejoined Ben and Laura in amongst the tumble of rocks.

'There were three of 'em,' he informed the twins.

'You . . . you killed all three?' exclaimed Ben, wide-eyed.

'With a li'l help from you,' said Stone. 'That was a nice shot of yourn took out one of 'em,' he commented.

'It was a lucky one,' replied Ben modestly.

'No, it wasn't. You're a darned good shot,' intervened his sister, anxious that Ben shouldn't put himself down.

'Anyways,' said Ben, 'it was Mr Stone saved us. If you hadn't happened to ride along . . . '

'Mebbe those varmints wouldn't've begun shootin',' said Stone.

'Whaddya mean?' enquired the youth.

'Wa'al, usually road agents hold up their victims, but those fellers jest began blastin' away at us without a word.'

'What are you sayin'?' asked Laura curiously.

'I figure they were out to kill, not to rob us. As I said earlier, we don't none of us look as though we're worth robbin'.'

'But . . . but why would they wanta kill us?' cried the girl.

'I'm only guessin', but, y'see, I recognized one of 'em. Bobcat Deevers. A low-down, no-good critter whose brother I shot a few years back in Dodge City. I was deppity marshal at the time an' Bobcat's brother was one of a gang who tried to rob the bank. There was one helluva shoot-out an', durin' the course of it, I plugged Jethro Deevers.'

'So, you think that this Bobcat Deevers was out for revenge?' said Ben.

'I guess so, though how in blue blazes he knew I was headin' this way the Lord knows!' Stone smiled wryly and continued, 'Seems like you two got caught up in this only 'cause you chanced to be ridin' along with me.'

'We don't know that for sure, Mr Stone,' said Laura.

'No, but it seems the most likely explanation.'

'I s'pose,' said Ben.

'Anyways, I apologize for involvin' you.'

There's nothin' to apologize about,' said Laura.

'No. It wasn't your fault. It was jest one of them things,' said Ben.

'It's said things run in threes,' remarked Laura. 'I jest hope there is no third shootin'.'

'What exactly are you talkin' about?' enquired a mystified Jack Stone.

'Last night in Mustang Pass we witnessed another shootin',' replied Laura.

'You did?'

'Yes.' Laura went on to describe the murder of Nathan B. Marston in the Grand Hotel, and she concluded by saying, 'The sheriff told us that the murdered man was the mayor of Boulder Creek, where we're headed.

Now ain't that a coincidence?'

'It sure is,' averred Stone. Then he smiled at the two youngsters and said, 'You've had a kinda unfortunate introduction to the state of Montana, but, b'lieve me, it can be a good place to live, I'm sure you'll like it up in Miller County.'

'Wa'al, I for one cain't wait to git there!' declared Ben.

'Me neither,' said Laura. 'I jest hope we like Uncle Henry an' he likes us.'

'Aw, you'll git along together fine!' stated Stone reassuringly. He took the Winchester from Ben and replaced it in his saddleboot. Then he swung into the saddle. 'Let's hit the road,' he growled.

'Yeah, let's,' said Ben.

The twins quickly mounted and all three set off once more. They proceeded at a brisk canter, their aim to reach Boulder Creek before darkness fell.

They made good time and, despite the delay occasioned by the ambush, reached the small cattle town as dusk was falling. They rode through Boulder Creek's Main Street until they found themselves opposite the law office. Thereupon, they promptly reined in their horses.

'I figure I'd best report what happened back on the trail to the local sheriff,' said Stone.

'We'll come with you,' said Ben. 'We can ask him for directions to the Big Canyon ranch.'

'Good idea!'

The Kentuckian dismounted and hitched the gelding to the rail outside the law office. Then, followed by two youngsters, he climbed up onto the stoop and proceeded to march into the office.

Inside, they found the sheriff behind his desk giving instructions to his deputy. Sheriff Joe Brand was a small, weasel-faced man in his late thirties, with cold, pebble-black eyes and a neat pencil-thin moustache above his thin lips. He was clad in a brown three-piece, city-style suit and he wore a

Remington tied down on his left thigh. His deputy, Tim Hollis, was a much younger man, tall and gangly-looking. He had an easy-going, amiable manner, with looks to match, and was rather less formally dressed, sporting a battered Stetson, check shirt, brown leather vest, Levis and well-worn brown leather boots. He also carried a Remington, but wore it tied down on his right thigh.

Both lawmen looked up as Stone and his two young companions approached the desk. The sheriff cut short his instructions.

'OK, Tim, you'd best git goin' on our rounds,' he snapped.

'Sure thing, Sheriff,' replied the deputy and, raising his hat in acknow-ledgement to the three newcomers, he hurried outside.

'Wa'al, what can I do for you folks?' enquired Sheriff Joe Brand.

'Firstly, I'd like to make a report,' said Stone, and he promptly went on to describe the attack and shoot-out on the trail.

When he had finished, Brand stared at him in silence for a few moments and then commented, 'You must be pretty goddam good with a gun, Mr . . . er . . . ?'

'Stone. Jack Stone.'

Brand stared harder than ever. He had, of course, heard of the Kentuckian. There would be few peace officers across the West who hadn't.

'Wa'al, I don't want no trouble here in Boulder Creek, Stone,' he rasped. 'This here's a peaceable kinda town.'

'That's fine by me,' replied Stone equably.

'You plannin' on stayin' long?'

'Nope. Jest overnight. I'm headin' for Great Falls.'

'Good!' The sheriff turned his attention to the youngsters, 'An' what about you two?' he demanded.

'We'd like directions to the Big Canyon Ranch, please,' said Ben politely.

'The Big Canyon? That's Henry Turpin's spread.'

'That's right. He's our uncle,' said Ben.

'Wow! Is that so?' exclaimed the sheriff.

'Yes. We've come to stay with him.'

'Yeah, yeah; I b'lieve he did say somethin' 'bout havin' a nephew an' niece comin' to stay. Your folks is dead, right?'

'Yes.'

'Wa'al, the Big Canyon lies a good five miles to the north-east of here.'

'That's not far.'

'No, it ain't, but it's gittin' pretty dark outside an' the trail's kinda tricky, with several forks along the way. You could easy miss your turnin'.'

'Couldn't you direct us?' asked Ben.

'Sure I could. 'Deed, I'll draw you a map. But I'd counsel you to wait until daybreak to follow it. You're much less likely to git lost when you can see where you're goin'. An' it's wild country out there. Ain't that so, Stone?'

The Kentuckian nodded.

'The sheriff's right. You'd do best to

stop over,' he said.

'But if the Big Canyon's only five miles off . . . '

'Let's do as the sheriff suggests,' intervened a weary-looking Laura. 'I'm dead beat an' if we do git lost . . . '

Ben glanced at his sister, observing how tired she looked, for the long ride and the trauma of the ambuscade had taken their toll. He determined, therefore, that it would be better, after all, to spend the night in town.

'OK, sis,' he said. 'We'll set out for Uncle Henry's ranch first thing in the mornin'. For tonight, can you recommend us any place we can stay?' he asked the sheriff.

'Try John Gordon's Grizzly Bear Hotel across the street,' suggested Brand.

It, like Mustang Pass's Grand Hotel, was the only hotel in town.

'Thank you.'

'I'll draw you that map, so's you don't take a wrong fork,' said Brand.

Again Ben Johnson thanked him.

Joe Brand quickly sketched the trail between Boulder Creek and the ranch. With its many forks, it would have been only too likely that the youngsters would have lost their way in the dark.

Having folded the map and placed it in his vest pocket, Ben thanked the sheriff a third time. Then he, his sister and Stone left the law office.

As Stone closed the door behind him, Sheriff Joe Brand rasped, 'Don't forgit, Stone, I don't want you causin' no trouble here in town.'

'I won't forgit,' replied the Kentuckian.

He noted that the sheriff deliberately failed to address him as 'mister', but he made no comment. Joe Brand was not the only lawman in the West to be uneasy at Stone's reputation and, in consequence, he wanted him out of town.

All three left their horses in the care of an ostler at the livery stables next to the hotel. Then they entered the Grizzly Bear and booked and paid for rooms for the night.

They supped together in the Grizzly Bear's dining-room and found, to their surprise, that the food was pretty good. Not that Laura ate much, for exhaustion had deprived her of her appetite. It was only mid-evening when bone-weary, she retired to her bed, leaving Stone and her brother sitting over their coffees.

'You weary, too, son?' enquired the Kentuckian.

No. Surprisin', ain't it, but I cain't say I am,' replied Ben.

'Wa'al, I was figurin' on moseyin' on over to one of the saloons an' havin' me a coupla beers,' said Stone.

'I . . . I ain't never drunk no beer,' confessed Ben. 'Ma said I was too young.'

'You fancy tryin' one now?'

'Yeah; I do, as a matter of fact.'

'Wa'al, I guess it won't do you no harm.'

'You invitin' me along, Mr Stone.'

'Yup. If 'n' you'd like to come?'

'I sure would.'

# 3

There were three saloons in town: McBain's, the Trail's End and the Ace of Diamonds. It was to the last-named that Jack Stone and Ben Johnson repaired.

The Ace of Diamonds was on the same side of Main Street as the hotel, but fifty yards further north. It was the largest and most profitable of the three establishments. Downstairs consisted of a large bar-room with a long, marble-topped bar down one side and at the far end, directly opposite the batwing doors, a small stage. Brass lamps hung from the rafters and the floor was spread with sweet-smelling sawdust. To reach either the bar or the stage, a customer had to wend his way between the tables and chairs that occupied virtually all of the floor-space.

During the week, many of these

tables would be empty, while games of poker or blackjack would be in progress at a number of those that were occupied. But tonight was Saturday night and the games of chance would begin later. When Stone and the seventeen-year-old stepped in through the batwing doors, every table and every chair in the bar-room was taken, for it was showtime. On Saturday nights, when the cowboys from the Big Canyon, Bar H and Lazy S ranches rode into town, the Ace of Diamonds presented a song-and-dance show. It was performed between the hours of eight and nine and starred the pro- prietor's blonde-haired wife, Dolly Swanley.

Not only were all the tables taken, there was a crowd three deep at the bar. Stone pushed his way through, followed by a wide-eyed Ben Johnson. Then, as the Kentuckian leant on the marbled bar-top and ordered two beers, the red plush curtains screening the stage parted to reveal the proprietor, Jim Swanley.

Swanley viewed his customers with a smug, self-satisfied smirk. He was large and fat and attired in a black city-style suit and derby hat. These were both of the finest materials, as was the sparkling white shirt which showed above his crimson-brocade vest. This stretched tightly over his enormous girth, while a neat black tie and highly polished black shoes completed the picture.

''Evenin', folks!' he cried. 'It's showtime!'

'Yippee!' yelled several of the cow-pokes present, and one, in his excitement, fired his Colt revolver into the air.

'No shootin', please!' barked Jim Swanley. 'We don't want no accidents. No, siree! So, jest sit back an' relax, an' prepare to enjoy the first-rate entertainment which it is my pleasure to present to you. Folks, I give you Dolly Swanley, Boulder Creek's very own nightingale, together with her lovely troupe of dancin' gals!'

This announcement brought forth loud cheers and rapturous applause, but no further shots, from the mixed bag of townsfolk, homesteaders and cowhands who had packed the Ace of Diamonds that evening.

Immediately, the band, consisting of Dick Dogerty the honky-tonk piano-player, Hal Archer the fiddler and Two Spoons Farren the spoons player, took up their positions in front of, and to one side of, the stage. This was the highlight of their week. Other days these musicians split up, Dick Dogerty playing at the Ace of Diamonds, while Hal Archer and Two Spoons Farren played at McBain's and the Trail's End respectively.

The band struck up and to even more thunderous applause Dolly Swanley and her troupe pranced from the wings onto the stage.

Dolly was a once-beautiful, yet still pretty, bottle-blonde in her mid-thirties. Although plumper than in her prime, Dolly had a fine body, with shapely arms and legs and a magnificent pair of breasts, which her low-cut blue-velvet gown did little to conceal.

Her troupe comprised the Ace of Diamonds's three sporting women, Arkansas Annie clad in dark green, Rio Rita in mauve and Wyoming Wendy in bright red. Their gowns were just as revealing as Dolly's, cut low at the bodice and shortened to expose their slender legs clad in fishnet stockings and gartered in the same hues as their gowns.

The performance was simple yet effective. Dolly had a pleasant, melodious voice and, while she entertained the audience with her rather limited repertoire of songs and ballads, the three sporting women joined in the choruses and executed their dance routines.

The dancing was energetic if nothing else, highkicks featuring frequently in each and every sequence, much to the delight of the Ace of Diamonds's customers. They whooped and hollered, whistled and yelled, as the girls kicked high to afford them a glimpse of their knickers or bent low to reveal their ample cleavages. Following the performance, the saloon's patrons would be queuing up to take the women upstairs and enjoy their favours. That was one reason why Jim Swanley put on the show. The other was his wife's obvious delight in performing on stage.

Jack Stone watched and listened, a wry smile playing upon his lips. He had viewed many such shows across the West and also, in his time, visited professional theatres in 'Frisco, Denver, Kansas City and Chicago. While Dolly Swanley and her dancers performed quite creditably, their show in no way measured up to those Stone had seen in 'Frisco and the other cities. He enjoyed it nevertheless, for, like all red-blooded males, he was naturally excited by the spectacle of voluptuous, scantily clad women prancing about on stage, exhibiting their charms.

Ben Johnson was no less excited. Indeed, the innocent, naïve youngster was utterly bowled over. He had seen nothing like this before. Completely oblivious of everything and everyone around him, his gaze rooted to the action on the stage, he left the bar and wended his way between the tables towards the performers. Stone grinned and followed.

Just as the seventeen-year-old and the Kentuckian reached the foremost tables shots rang out.

The first shattered the beer-glass in Ben's hand, the second whipped his low-crowned black Stetson from his head and the third and fourth both whistled past Stone's left cheek, so close he felt the wind from them.

Straightaway, the Kentuckian tipped the nearest table over and dragged Ben down behind it. Nearby tables and chairs toppled over, too, as the customers dived for cover.

Half a dozen more shots rained down and pandemonium ensued, some people dropping to the floor, while others attempted to flee from the saloon. The performers, conscious of their vulnerable position, leapt from the stage. Dolly Swanley fell on top of her husband and, consequently, was afforded a very soft landing indeed. Wyoming Wendy and Arkansas Annie both had their fall broken by Dick Dogerty. Then all three scrambled behind the piano. Rio Rita ended up entwined with Two Spoons Farren, so entangled they could have been one. As for the fiddler, Hal Archer, he threw himself down beside Jack Stone and Ben Johnson.

'What in tarnation's goin' on?' he demanded, as another couple of shots thudded into the table behind which he was cowering.

'I dunno, but I aim to find out,' muttered Stone.

He peered cautiously round the edge of the table. Opposite, and directly across the bar-room from the bar, a flight of wooden steps ran up to the upper storey. A small railed balcony led from the head of this stairway to the bedrooms where the saloon's sporting women entertained their clients. And it was from the balcony that the shots had come. Two gunmen crouched there, their revolvers trained on the crowd beneath and their eyes desperately searching for their intended victim.

'Who in blazes are those varmints shootin' at?' enquired Hal Archer.

'It could be me,' said Stone.

'Like it was back on the trail?' said Ben.

'Yeah, though I don't recognize either of 'em.'

'There are two shootists, are there?' asked Ben, not daring to peek.

'Yup.'

'So, what are you gonna do?'

'Go git 'em, I s'pose,' said Stone.

For a big man, the Kentuckian moved surprisingly quickly. He drew his Frontier Model Colt, leapt up and, blazing away at the men on the balcony, charged across the bar-room towards the stairway. He kicked aside chairs and leapt over recumbent forms as he proceeded headlong in the direction of the two gunslingers. Nothing and nobody was going to stop him from reaching them.

Clattering up the stairs, Stone aimed and fired his fifth shot. The others had missed their mark, but this found its target. The slug ripped into the nearer of the two gunmen's chest, sending him crashing backwards into the wall behind him. His confederate, unnerved by Stone's rampaging run, turned and fled along the upstairs corridor, on either side of which were the saloon's bedrooms.

Stone reached the balcony and confronted the stricken assassin. The man, a large, unshaven ruffian in cowpoke's gear, stared up at the Kentuckian and attempted to raise his Colt Peacemaker. But he had no chance, Stone's Frontier Model Colt was already aimed at him. Stone squeezed the trigger and blasted the man's brains out.

Then, reloading as he ran, Stone set

off along the corridor in pursuit of the second shootist. The man would, indeed should, have escaped, but for the fact that he could not shift the window at the far end of the corridor. It was stuck fast.

'Goddamit!' he yelled, abandoning his efforts to open the window and turning to face the Kentuckian.

That was the last word he uttered, for, as he turned, Stone, having finished reloading, fired. Once; twice; thrice. The slugs thudded into the gunman's chest and sent him flying backwards through that very window which he had so desperately been trying to open.

Stone hurried forward and peered down into the street below. The man lay spread-eagled in the dust while a crowd gathered round him. They consisted mainly of those who had fled from the saloon when the shooting began. Satisfied that the second would-be assassin was also dead, Stone turned and retraced his steps.

When eventually he reached the foot of the stairway, he found not only Ben Johnson and Jim and Dolly Swanley waiting to greet him, but also Sheriff Joe Brand, who, roused by the sound of the shooting, had come hot-foot from the law office. The sheriff was the first to speak.

'For Chrissake, Stone, what the hell's goin' on? You intent on shootin' up the whole of Boulder Creek?'

'Now wait a minute — ' began Stone.

'No; you wait a minute,' rasped Joe Brand. 'You ain't in town more 'n a coupla hours an' you've shot dead two of its citizens!'

'Some citizens!' exclaimed Stone. 'They tried to gun me down while I was jest standin' watchin' the show.'

'Aw, come on! Why would they do that? You pick a quarrel with 'em or somethin'?' demanded Brand.

'No, I did not. Like I said, I was jest watchin' the show an' they opened fire.'

'That's right, Sheriff,' cried Ben.

'They did. From up there, on that balcony.'

'They're tellin' the truth, Joe. That's how it happened,' concurred Dolly Swanley. 'Ain't that so, Jim?' she murmured to her husband.

'It is,' agreed the saloonkeeper. 'They opened fire without warnin'.'

Joe Brand scowled. This was not what he wanted to hear. He had wanted a good reason either to arrest Stone or run him out of town.

'But why would they wanta gun down a complete stranger?' He turned to Stone. 'You don't know 'em, do you?' he growled.

'Nope. Never saw 'em before in my life,' said Stone.

'Wally an' Willy Gregg. Coupla ne'er-do-wells, but lived in these parts all their lives,' said Jim Swanley.

'It don't seem to make no sense,' added Dolly.

'Wa'al, anyways, you sure attract trouble, Stone,' commented Brand sourly. 'First of all you're ambushed along the trail an' now you nearly git yourself assassinated here in the Ace of Diamonds!'

'It's a mystery,' confessed Stone.

'Yeah. Wa'al, I like things nice an' quiet, so I want you outa this town pronto.'

'I'll leave in the mornin' when I'm good an' ready,' replied Stone. Eyeing the sheriff coldly, he enquired, 'You got any objection to that, Sheriff?'

Joe Brand continued to scowl. He could think of no reason to justify running the Kentuckian out of town earlier. He shrugged his shoulders and muttered reluctantly, 'No objection.'

'Good!' Stone glanced round. The crowd had for the most part returned to the saloon, and a path had been opened through which the body of Wally Gregg was being conveyed. He and his brother were both destined to be laid out in the funeral parlour. 'I figure you an' me'll have another beer, huh, Ben?' said the Kentuckian.

'Yessir,' said Ben.

The youngster had never known such excitement. His eyes twinkled. Far from being frightened, he found he was actually enjoying his adventure, though he was relieved that his sister wasn't present.

'What about the show?' demanded a cowpoke from the Bar H.

'Yeah, what about the show?' echoed several others.

Jim Swanley glanced at his wife. She, in turn, glanced at the saloon-girls and the musicians who, having dusted themselves down, were grouped together round Dick Dogerty's piano.

'Quite right!' she said brightly. 'The show must go on!'

And, minutes later, it did.

# 4

Early the following morning Nathan B. Marston returned home to rest. His body was conveyed in a hearse drawn by two coal-black mares and driven by Horace Blundell, the mortician at Mustang Pass. Marston's untimely demise in another town had done Boulder Creek's mortician out of what he considered to be his rightful commission. But such was life, or, in this case, death.

Horace Blundell had made arrangements for the mayor's body to lie in state in the town hall until Monday morning, when the funeral was due to take place. It being Sunday there were several people on their way to church when the hearse proceeded into town and drew up in front of the town hall.

Among those who gathered round

the hearse were Sheriff Joe Brand, Doc Harris, the town's elderly physician, and John Gordon, Boulder Creek's deputy mayor and owner of the Grizzly Bear Hotel. They were soon joined by the lawyer, Vernon Oakridge, the banker, Hiram Goodge, and the blacksmith, Ned Taken.

'Holy cow! That . . . that's Nathan lyin' there dead!' exclaimed Doc Harris, peering into the hearse.

'What!' cried the lawyer, Vernon Oakridge.

'But Nathan's in Mustang Pass. Went there on business,' said John Gordon.

'That's where I jest brought him from,' retorted Horace Blundell.

'That's right.' Sheriff Joe Brand turned and faced the others. 'I got a wire from Jake Lucas yesterday. Seems some thief broke into the mayor's hotel room while he was sleepin'. (Lucas had tactfully made no mention in his telegram of Kate Kelly's presence in the room.) 'Unfortunately, the mayor woke up an' the thief went an' shot him.'

'Was the thief apprehended?' enquired Oakridge.

'Nope. He got clean away.'

'Why in tarnation didn't you inform me of this straightaway, Joe? I'm deputy mayor, for Pete's sake!' cried John Gordon angrily.

'Wa'al, y'see, it was like this . . . ' began Brand, when he was suddenly interrupted by none other than Nathan B. Marston's cousin and next of kin, Earl Peplow.

Peplow, who owned a run-down homestead two miles out of town, had at that moment ridden into Boulder Creek on his grey mare and, upon spying the hearse, cried out, 'Is that . . . is that Cousin Nathan?'

'Yeah, Earl, it is,' said the sheriff.

'You knew Nathan was dead?' enquired John Gordon.

'Sure. Joe rode over an' told me yesterday,' replied Peplow.

The hotelier turned to confront the sheriff.

'But you didn't think to tell me,

Nathan's deppity an' your brother-in-law!' he remarked.

'I was gonna explain the reason for that,' said Joe Brand. 'Y'see, I didn't git Jake Lucas's wire till late yesterday afternoon, on account of havin' been away on the far side of the county investigatin' a reported rustlin'. When I did git to read the wire, I naturally rode out to Earl's place an' informed him as next of kin. Then I broke the sad news to his intended, Widow Morgan.'

'So, why didn't you step round from Widow Morgan's house to the Grizzly Bear? We ain't that far apart,' said Gordon.

'No, you ain't,' agreed Brand. 'But by then it was time to give young Tim his instructions. An' the arrival of Henry Turpin's nephew and niece meant that — '

'Oh, so, they've arrived at last! Henry's been expectin' 'em for some days now,' said Hiram Goodge.

'Wa'al, they rode in with a feller

named Jack Stone, an ex-lawman. Guess they must've been in Mustang Pass the night Nathan got shot.'

'Nephew an' niece, y'say? How . . . how old would they be?' enquired Peplow.

' 'Bout sixteen, seventeen,' said Brand.

'Did you direct 'em to the Big Canyon?' asked Ned Taken, the black-smith.

'Nope. Figured they could easily lose their way in the dark. Suggested they stop the night at the Grizzly Bear.'

'That's right,' averred the hotelier. 'They an' that Stone feller are still there in the hotel. Though this doesn't explain, Joe why — '

'I'm comin' to that,' said the sheriff irritably. 'By this time, I was more'n ready for somethin' to eat. So, I aimed to pop along an' give you the news of Nathan's death directly after supper. Only there was that shootin' at the Ace of Diamonds, an' I guess that jest blew all thought of poor Nathan's death clean outa my head.'

'I see.'

'Sorry, John, but that's the way it was.'

'Anyways,' said Earl Peplow, 'what are the plans for Nathan's funeral?'

'Wa'al, sir,' said Horace Blundell, the mortician, 'since yo're the next of kin, I reckon it's up to you to say what you want doin'. But, unless you've got any objections, I propose to lay your cousin out in the town hall. Then, perhaps you an' me can speak with the preacher an' fix up the funeral for sometime tomorrow mornin'? 'Course we'll have to wait till after mornin' service 'fore we approach him.'

'That'll be fine. Meantime, I'll jest go hitch my hoss to the rail in front of the Trail's End,' said Peplow, and, without more ado, he trotted off in the direction of the saloon.

'Yeah. An', if 'n' the rest of us are aimin' to attend mornin' service, we'd best mosey along,' said Hiram Googe.

''Deed we had,' agreed John Gordon, after consulting his pocket watch.

As the crowd was dispersing Jack Stone and his two young friends emerged on the stoop in front of the Grizzly Bear Hotel. The Kentuckian was intending to head for the general store, to pick up sufficient provisions for the remainder of his journey to Great Falls, while Ben and Laura proposed to retrieve their horses from the livery stables and, with the help of Sheriff Joe Brand's hand-drawn map, follow the trail to the Big Canyon ranch.

'Wa'al, I guess this is where we part,' said Stone. 'I sure hope things quieten down now an' you git on OK with your uncle.'

'So do we,' said Ben.

'Yeah; we've had quite enough excitement for a while,' added Laura. 'What with the ambush on the trail, last night's shoot-out at the saloon an', before that, the murder I witnessed back in Mustang Pass.'

'Talkin' of which, that could well be the victim's corpse in the hearse over there,' said Ben, glancing across the street.

'Why d'you say that?' asked Stone.

'Wa'al, it would've taken 'bout this time to transport the corpse here from Mustang Pass.'

'I guess it would at that.' Stone studied the hearse with interest and then, turning again to his two young friends, declared, 'Anyways, I'd best go git those provisions I need. So, good luck to you both.'

'Thanks, Mr Stone,' replied Ben.

'Yeah; thanks,' echoed Laura.

They all three shook hands and then Stone headed for the general store while the twins made their way towards the livery stables.

The youngsters paid their dues, mounted their horses and trotted out of the stables, back onto Main Street. Across the street, Horace Blundell and his assistant were manoeuvring the coffin containing the mayor's corpse up onto the stoop in front of the town hall. And, having hitched his horse to the rail

70

outside the Trail's End saloon, Earl Peplow was strolling nonchalantly along the sidewalk towards the town hall. He spotted Ben and Laura at the same moment that Laura spotted him. Their eyes met. Each recognized the other.

'Oh, holy cow!' exclaimed Laura.

'What's the matter, sis?' asked Ben.

'It . . . it's him!'

'It's who?'

'Him! The man who shot the mayor back in Mustang Pass!'

'What! Where?'

'Over there. Across the street.'

Ben followed his sister's pointing finger, but, as he did so, Peplow turned abruptly on his heel and headed back towards the Trail's End. Consequently, Ben was quite unable to identify him as the gunman he had clashed with in the Grand Hotel. Not that he had a clear picture of the man anyway, for it had been dark in the hotel corridor and, unlike Laura, he had not succeeded in obtaining a good look at the man's face.

'Are . . . are you sure it's him?' he enquired.

'Yes, Ben, I'm sure.'

'Gee!'

'So, what shall we do? Go find the sheriff?'

'No. Let's do what we planned to do, an' ride on out to the Big Canyon. We can tell Uncle Henry an' see what he's gotta say.'

'But Ben . . . '

'If 'n' you're right, Laura, an' that feller is the shootist, then I figure the sooner we lam outa town the better. S'pose he finds us 'fore we find the sheriff? He's mebbe gone to fetch his gang.'

'I hadn't thought of that,' confessed Laura nervously.

'So, let's git goin'.'

'OK, Ben.'

The two youngsters dug their heels into their horses' flanks and set off at a gallop. They aimed to follow the trail north-eastwards, using the sheriff's map to avoid taking any wrong forks. A ride of a mere five miles would take them to the safety of their uncle's ranch.

Earl Peplow, meantime, had reached the Trail's End saloon. He dived in through the batwing doors and hurried over to a corner table where sat two of his drinking cronies. Bill Hudson and Jed Burke owned the homestead next to his own. Their farm was, if anything, even more run-down than Peplow's. Both men were in their mid-thirties, tough-looking, sturdily built men in check shirts and Levis. Hudson boasted a thick black beard, while Burke was merely unshaven. They each carried a Colt Peacemaker.

'Boys, I need your help,' said Peplow, without preamble.

The two men stared up at Peplow's hawklike visage and noted the murderous gleam in his cold, steely blue eyes.

'Yeah? What's goin' on?' enquired Bill Hudson.

'I cain't explain now, 'cause I've gotta go speak with the mortician an' the preacher.'

'Oh, yeah; we heard 'bout Nathan!' said Jed Burke. 'You have our sympathy, Earl; don't he, Bill?'

''Course. Why I — '

'Never mind that now. Jest lissen. OK?'

'OK.'

'Right. There's a coupla youngsters, a boy an' a gal, both 'bout sixteen, seventeen. They're this moment ridin' outa town an' headin' for Henry Turpin's Big Canyon ranch. Wa'al, I want you to pursue 'em an' stop 'em.'

'What! But why in blue blazes . . . ?' began Hudson.

'But . . . but what do we do with 'em once we've stopped 'em?' asked Burke.

'Shoot 'em.'

'Oh, no! I ain't never killed nobody an' I don't aim to. They hang you for that in this state!' cried Burke.

'That's right!' averred Hudson.

'OK! OK! Jest grab 'em an' take 'em back to my place. Lock 'em in my barn an' we'll decide what to do with 'em when I git there.'

'An' when will that be, Earl?' growled Hudson.

'Jest as soon as I'm finished arrangin' Nathan's funeral,' said Peplow.

'But why in hell should we oblige you in this matter? If 'n' things go wrong . . . '

'They won't, Bill. An' I'll pay you well, real well.'

'But you ain't got no . . . ' Jed Burke paused and pondered. Suddenly, his eyes lit up and he exclaimed, ' 'Course, you bein' Nathan's only relative, guess you inherit everythin'! Jeeze, Earl, you've jest become the richest man in the whole of Miller County!'

'That's right. So, if 'n' you want a share of them there riches, you'd best git goin'. Your quarry's got a substantial lead on you, an', unless you git to 'em 'fore they reach the Big Canyon, you ain't gonna git nothin'.'

The two homesteaders exchanged glances.

'OK,' said Jed Burke. 'We'll do it.'

'See you both back at my place,' said Peplow.

Burke and Hudson rose, and all three hurried out through the batwing doors. Once outside, Burke and Hudson quickly mounted their horses and set off in pursuit of the youngsters. Earl Peplow watched them go. He prayed they would catch up with Ben and Laura before they arrived at the ranch. He wasn't sure whether Ben could identify him as his cousin's killer, but he had no doubt that Laura could. And he had no wish to end his days dancing at the end of a rope.

Ben and Laura should have reached the Big Canyon before Earl Peplow's accomplices caught up with them. Had they been familiar with the trail, they certainly would have done so. But they were not familiar with it and, in consequence, made frequent halts to consult Sheriff Joe Brand's map.

And so it was that they were about half a mile from their destination when they were overtaken by Bill

Hudson and Jed Burke.

The two homesteaders galloped past the twins, then wheeled round their horses, reined them in and blocked the youngsters' passage.

'Hold on there!' yelled Hudson.

The youngsters in turn reined in their horses.

'Will you please let us past?' said Ben, eyeing the two men nervously.

''Fraid not,' said Hudson.

'But . . . but why not?' enquired the youth.

''Cause we want you to come with us,' replied Hudson.

'Wa'al, we ain't comin'. We are headin' for the Big Canyon ranch an' you're not gonna stop us!' cried Ben.

'Oh, yes, we are!' interjected Burke, drawing his revolver and aiming it at the boy.

The colour faded from Ben's cheeks and Laura began to cry. She had recently been through one ordeal after another and this latest unexpected hold-up was more than she could take.

'Quit snivellin' an' git movin',' snarled Jed Burke.

'Yeah. Take that fork over there, an' be quick about it,' added Bill Hudson, indicating a narrow track which branched off to the right.

'But — '

'Do as you're told, boy, or I shoot,' said Burke.

Reluctantly, Ben turned his horse's head.

'Come on, sis,' he whispered.

'But, Ben, what are these men gonna do with us?' sobbed Laura.

'I dunno, Laura. Guess we'll soon find out.'

So saying, Ben trotted off along the narrow track. Laura followed, with the two homesteaders bringing up the rear. Jed Burke continued to brandish his Colt Peacemaker, in case either of the twins tried to make a run for it.

They had scarcely vanished from view when six riders appeared upon the trail, coming from the direction of the Big Canyon and heading towards town.

The leader was a tall, lean man in his early forties. He had cool blue eyes and a strong-jawed, weather-beaten face, and there was an air of authority about him. This was not surprising, since he ran the biggest, most successful ranch in Miller County. Henry Turpin was not best pleased. An accident to a colt had delayed his departure from the Big Canyon and, as a result, he was likely to be late for church. He, his foreman Max Wayne, a rawboned, blond-haired thirty-year-old, and those four of his hands who had expressed a wish to accompany him to morning service were all attired in their Sunday best. Their fast gallop, however, was likely to result in their arriving in Boulder Creek somewhat dustladen.

On this particular Sunday, Henry Turpin had not only church in mind as he rode towards the town. He was also thinking of his nephew and niece, whom he was expecting to arrive at any moment.

# 5

Jack Stone quickly discovered that Boulder Creek's shops and stores did not open on a Sunday. The God-fearing community did their best to keep the Sabbath holy. At least, to a point. The hotel and the town's three saloons remained open for business. Indeed, not a few of its citizens repaired to one or other of these establishments immediately after attending church. And some of its citizens repaired thence instead of attending church. One such was Bob Butler, the proprietor of the general store. A small, wiry, grey-haired, bespectacled fellow, he was engaged in his usual Sunday morning poker-game, with five cronies in the Trail's End, when Stone eventually found him.

The Kentuckian had buttonholed Deputy Sheriff Tim Hollis to ask why the general store was closed, had been given an explanation and pointed in the direction of the saloon with the remark, 'Bob'll likely slip you in the back door an' tend to your needs, for he ain't the kinda feller to miss out on a sale. No, siree!'

Stone strolled across to the bar, ordered a beer and asked the bartender, 'Is Mr Bob Butler on these premises?'

The bartender eyed Stone curiously.

'Who wants to know?' he rasped.

'I do, or I wouldn't be askin',' replied Stone, allowing a certain edge to creep into his voice.

The bartender glanced a second time at the Kentuckian. He had intended saying, 'An' jest who are you?', but the look in Stone's eyes warned him that this would not be wise. Instead, he glanced across at the poker players and said, 'The li'l filler wearin' the specs an' the brown derby hat; that's Bob Butler.'

'Thanks.'

Stone took a swig of his beer, then carrying the glass, made his way to the table where the poker game was in progress. He watched and waited until they had completed the hand they were playing.

'Mr Bob Butler?' he said, eyeing the storekeeper.

Butler looked up at the big Kentuckian.

'Yes, that's me. What can I do for you, stranger?' he asked.

'I was hopin' you might open up your store,' said Stone.

'We don't open on the Sabbath. It's agin' the town ordinances.'

'Yeah, but I git the impression that the law round here turns a blind eye providin' yo're discreet.' Stone smiled and continued, 'I'm headin' up north an' jest want a few provisions. I wouldn't take more 'n a few minutes of your time.'

Bob Butler's eyes glinted behind his wire-framed spectacles. The deputy had spoken the truth. The storekeeper was not a man to pass up on a sale, however small.

'OK,' he said. 'I s'pose we can slip in through the back door.' He rose and turned to his fellow poker-players. 'You'll have to excuse me, boys. Guess I'll miss the next coupla hands, but I'll be back.'

With these words, Bob Butler headed for the batwing doors. Stone hastily threw back the remains of his beer and followed the little man out onto Main Street.

As they made their way towards the general store they passed the town hall. The hearse still stood outside.

'Poor ol' Nathan!' cried Butler, shaking his head sorrowfully.

'Your mayor?'

'Yup.'

'Gunned down by some goddam thief in some hotel in Mustang Pass, so I'm told.'

'Yup. A bad business. I feel particularly sorry for Jane Morgan.'

'Oh, yeah?'

'Yup. A widder-woman here in town. She an' Nathan were plannin' to git hitched. 'Deed, he confided in me that, jest as soon as he finished his business over in Mustang Pass, he an' the widder would git together an' set a date for their weddin'.'

'She must be real cut up.'

'You're right there. An' I s'pose Earl's pretty cut up too, though, 'course, he's set to inherit.'

'Earl?'

'Earl Peplow; Nathan's cousin an' only livin' kin. He'll inherit everythin', I guess.'

'So, the widow Morgan misses out.'

'Aw, it wasn't Nathan's money an' property she was after. It was Nathan hisself. She's pretty well-heeled an', had they married, I reckon they'd've owned practically the whole of Boulder Creek between them.'

'Includin' your store?'

'Yup. I rent the property off'n Nathan.'

'An' is Earl Peplow a man of property?'

'Wa'al, in a manner of speakin'. He's

a homesteader. Has a place out near the Big Canyon. It's pretty run-down, so I guess Earl's feelin' of sadness at his cousin's demise will be somewhat lessened by the thought of his inheritance.'

'S'pose so.'

'Anyways, here we are. Let's slip round the back.'

They climbed down off the sidewalk and turned into a narrow alleyway between the store and the barbering parlour. A short flight of wooden steps led up to the rear door. Bob Butler quickly unlocked this and they went inside.

Jack Stone's needs were soon met: some coffee, some hardtack and a quantity of beef jerky. The Kentuckian stumped up and they left the store by the same door through which they had entered. Thereupon, the little storekeeper retraced his steps to the Trail's End saloon, while Stone headed for the livery stables.

Stone, having saddled the gelding and placed his provisions in the saddlebags, trotted out of the stables and into Main Street. As he did so, he espied Henry Turpin, his foreman and four hands riding into town.

'As we're plumb late already, we'd best head straight for the church,' said Turpin to his men. 'We can make enquiries 'bout Ben an' Laura after the service.'

The rancher's words carried to the ears of the Kentuckian. Immediately, he positioned the gelding in the path of the oncoming horsemen.

'You wouldn't be Henry Turpin, by any chance?' he said.

'I would,' replied the rancher, reining in his black stallion. 'An' who would you be, stranger?'

'My name's Jack Stone. I'm jest passin' through.'

'So, why'd you wanta know who I am?'

'You mentioned Ben an' Laura, your nephew an' niece.'

'How'd you know they're my nephew an' niece?'

'I met 'em on the trail 'tween Mustang Pass an' here. We rode along together an' got to talkin'.'

'I see.'

'You spoke 'bout makin' enquiries regardin' them.'

'Yeah.'

'You jest rode in from your ranch?'

'That's right.'

'Wa'al, didn't you run across 'em on the trail?'

'Nope.'

'That's strange. They rode outa here 'bout twenty, thirty minutes ago, aimin' to take the trail to the Big Canyon ranch.'

'That's my place all right.'

'Mebbe they took a wrong fork,' interjected Max Wayne.

'Yeah. It's easy done,' added Buck Walters, one of the cowhands, a snub-nosed, red-headed twenty-year-old with a perpetual grin and a mischievous glint in his eye.

'Ben had a map drawn for him by the sheriff,' said Stone.

'Wa'al, Joe Brand knows this country like the back of his hand,' remarked Max Wayne, the foreman.

'So, any map drawn by him should be pretty goddam accurate,' mused Henry Turpin.

'Mebbe you oughta speak with him, boss?' suggested Buck Walters.

'He'll be where we're headin',' said Wayne.

'Yeah. Wa'al, we can hardly go interruptin' the mornin' service,' growled Turpin. 'I mean, Ben an' Laura may have found their way again an' be at the Big Canyon by this time.'

'Shall I ride back an' check?' asked Buck Walters eagerly.

'Yeah, you do that, Buck,' said Turpin. 'The rest of us, meanwhile, will slip into the pews at the back of the church, attend what remains of the service, an' then have a word with Joe.'

'I'll come with you,' volunteered Stone, for he had grown fond of the two youngsters and his instincts told him that something was badly amiss. He could not have said why, yet he had a nasty feeling that they had not simply misread the sheriff's map and taken a wrong turning.

The church service was one-third over by the time the six of them arrived and found seats in the rearmost pew. Nevertheless, it seemed an age before the final hymn was sung and the congregation trooped out into the street. Mention of the mayor's death, followed by a lengthy peroration and then an announcement of the funeral arrangements had combined to extend the length of the service.

They were the first out and they waited impatiently for the sheriff to emerge. Consequently, he had barely finished exchanging a few words with the preacher before Henry Turpin accosted him.

'Mornin', Joe.'

'Mornin', Henry. You want somethin'?' asked the sheriff perceptively.

'Yeah. My nephew an' niece. Mr Stone here tells me that you drew 'em a map showin' how to git to the Big Canyon.'

The sheriff surveyed Stone with a cold, hostile eye.

'That's right,' he said.

'You didn't miss off any forks in the trail?'

'No, Henry, I can assure you I didn't. That map was good an' accurate,' declared Brand.

'Hmm. Wa'al, Mr Stone tells me that they left town 'bout half an hour 'fore we rode in. So, it's kinda odd me an' the boys didn't run into 'em.'

'Yeah, I s'pose it is.' Joe Brand scratched his head. 'The map was pretty easy to follow. I don't really see how they could've taken a wrong turnin'.'

'OK. Wa'al, thanks, Joe. Reckon we'd best go look for 'em,' said Turpin.

'I'll ride with you an', if necessary, help you look,' said Stone.

'I don't think so,' snapped Brand. 'I want you outa this county.'

Henry Turpin shot an enquiring

glance at the sheriff.

'Why shouldn't Mr Stone help us look for 'em?' he demanded.

''Cause Stone's trouble, that's why. Hell, he hadn't been in town more 'n a few hours when he shot two of our citizens stone dead!'

'They started the shootin',' replied Stone evenly.

'That's as mebbe. I still want you — '

'Goddam it, Joe!' exploded Turpin. 'If Stone ain't broke no laws an' he wants to help, then, by God, you're gonna let him!'

Brand scowled. Henry Turpin was a man of considerable influence in Miller County and there were elections due in October. He could not, therefore, afford to alienate the rancher.

'OK! OK!' he muttered. Then, turning to the Kentuckian, he said in a reproving tone, 'I don't expect no more trouble from you, Stone.'

Jack Stone grinned.

'I'll be on my best behaviour, Sheriff,' he replied jocosely.

'You'd better be,' growled Brand.

Thereupon, while the sheriff stomped off towards the law office, Turpin, Stone and the others mounted their horses and headed in the direction of the Big Canyon ranch.

They were half-way there when they encountered Buck Walters. He looked rather glum.

'There ain't no sign of your nephew an' niece at the ranch,' he announced.

'Hell!' Henry Turpin glowered darkly. 'OK,' he said, 'let's make for the Big Canyon an' dig out the rest of the boys. Then we'll split up an' quarter the Big Canyon an' the plains an' hills surroundin' it. If 'n' we don't find 'em by dusk, we'll head back to the ranch an' decide what to do next.'

'We'll find 'em 'fore then,' said Buck Walters, with the eternal optimism of youth.

'I sure hope so,' said Turpin.

Back at the Big Canyon, they paired off, Henry Turpin assigning a particular stretch of country for each couple to scour. He sent them to the north and to the east of the ranch house, since, if the youngsters had followed Joe Brand's map, they almost certainly would have turned eastward off the main trail. Turpin assumed, therefore, that they had somehow missed the Big Canyon fork, ridden on northwards and then branched off eastward.

Jack Stone found he had the young, red-headed Buck Walters as his companion. The cowhand knew the terrain pretty well and they left no ravine, gulch, gully, hollow, arroyo or patch of sagebrush in their stretch unsearched. They went through each and every one methodically and thoroughly. But they found neither the twins nor any trace that they had passed that way.

Finally, as the light began to fade, they made their weary way back to the ranch. They were the last to return. Henry Turpin and the rest of his men were standing disconsolately in front of the cookhouse as they rode up.

'No luck?' said Turpin.

'None,' replied Stone.

The rancher rubbed his jaw and sighed heavily.

'Wa'al, we cain't do no more today,' he growled. 'I'll needs attend Nathan's funeral tomorrow, but I'll be askin' you to set out again at first light. Meantime, you boys enjoy your supper.'

'You figure we'll need to cast our net a li'l wider?' enquired the foreman, Max Wayne.

'I guess so,' replied Turpin. Then, addressing the Kentuckian, he said, 'You care to join tomorrow's search, Mr Stone?'

'I surely would,' said Stone.

'Then, you'd best come an' sup with me an' stay the night,' declared the rancher.

It was tradition at the Big Canyon that Henry Turpin dined alone in the ranch house, attended by his elderly Cheyenne cook and housekeeper, while Max Wayne and the rest of the hands ate in the cookhouse. That night, though, Turpin had Jack Stone for company.

They had an excellent beef stew cooked for them by the elderly Cheyenne, and, as they ate, so they talked. Turpin related how he had come West and worked as a roustabout, a wrangler and a trail-boss before settling in Miller County and slowly building up the ranch until it became one of the biggest spreads in all Montana. Stone, for his part, told the rancher of his early days in Kentucky and of how his father had been forced to sell off the family homestead to pay his gambling debts.

'Shortly afterwards,' Stone said, 'he was killed in a saloon brawl. Followin' that, my mother struggled, alone an' unaided, to bring me up. When she died, worn out by her efforts, I was jest fourteen years old. I've been on my own pretty much ever since.'

Stone did not, however, mention his brief marriage and how, within the first year of the marriage, his young wife had died in childbirth. The devastating effect of this tragic event had made him what he was: a man who would always be moving on, always looking for another frontier to cross.

'You've had it pretty tough, Mr Stone,' commented Turpin.

The big Kentuckian shrugged his shoulders.

'Life ain't easy, but we git by,' he drawled.

'Guess so.' Turpin smiled and added, 'Sheriff Joe Brand wasn't none too keen on your bein' in town.'

'Nope. I made quite a few enemies over the years. Most lawmen do.'

'You ain't still a lawman, though?'

'Nope. I retired. That doesn't, of course, prevent some folks bearin' a grudge an' tryin' to git even. A coupla fellers tried to plug me in the Ace of Diamonds, only I got them first. But the sheriff wasn't too happy. Seems he likes a quiet life.'

'Wa'al, you cain't exactly blame him for that.'

'Nope.'

'Who were these two fellers who tried to plug you?'

'A coupla local boys. Wally an' Willy Gregg.'

'How come they held a grudge agin' you?'

'Beats me.'

'You ain't never met 'em before?'

'Nope.'

'It's a mystery, then.'

'Sure is. Jest like the disappearance of your nephew an' niece.'

'Yeah.' Turpin pulled a wry face. 'I cain't think how we didn't find 'em.'

'Your foreman said mebbe we'd need to extend the limits of our search.'

'Yeah, I s'pose, though I wouldn't't've thought those two youngsters could've gotten any further than the area we searched today.'

'Wa'al, what other explanation can there be? They certainly set out for the Big Canyon this mornin'.'

'Yup.'

'So, they should've got here. Even if they misread the sheriff's map, surely they would've eventually realized their mistake an' backtracked?'

'It is a goddam mystery.'

'Wa'al, let's hope we find 'em tomorrow.'

'Yeah. It's a pity I've got Nathan's funeral to attend. I'll git away as soon as I decently can.'

'Mebbe, by the time you git back to the ranch, Ben an' Laura will already have been found?'

'Mebbe.'

The two men prayed that this would be so, although neither expected such a quick and happy outcome. They both feared that Ben and Laura had not simply missed their way, that something had happened to them. But, as to what that something could be, they had no idea.

# 6

Earl Peplow returned from town shortly after Henry Turpin began the search for his two missing relatives. Peplow had arranged with the mortician and the preacher that the funeral of his cousin should take place at nine o' clock on the following morning. He had succeeded in button-holing the preacher immediately prior to the commencement of the morning service, thereby allowing the preacher to announce the funeral arrangements during the course of the service.

Peplow found Jed Burke sitting smoking a cheroot in his, Peplow's rocking-chair on the front porch of his farmhouse. Of Bill Hudson and the twins there was no sign. Peplow dismounted and stepped up onto the porch.

'Where are those darned kids?' he demanded.

'Locked up safe an' sound in your barn, like you told us to,' replied Burke.

'An' Bill?'

'He's busy workin'.'

'On your farm?'

''Course on our farm. You didn't think he'd be workin' on yourn, did you?'

'Nope, I guess not.'

'I'll go fetch him. We got things to discuss.'

'OK. I'll take a look in the barn.'

'No. You stay right here, Earl. I don't want you goin' near them youngsters till we've had our talk.'

Peplow stared hard at his neighbour, but Burke did not waver. He simply stared straight back. Realizing that the other was determined, Peplow smiled sourly and shrugged his shoulders.

'OK. I'll stay here on the porch till you git back,' he promised.

Burke rose and, taking his place in the rocking-chair, Peplow proceeded to light a large cigar. Burke, meantime, tossed aside the dog-end of his cheroot, mounted his horse and rode off in the direction of his farm.

Earl Peplow was as good as his word, and, when eventually Jed Burke returned with Bill Hudson, the two found him still sitting patiently in the rocking-chair. He had by now lit up a second cigar and was sipping a glass of whiskey. The bottle and two empty glasses stood on the floor beside the rocking-chair. Peplow bent over and poured two generous measures. He offered the glasses to his two accomplices.

'Here you are, boys. This ain't no moonshine. This is reg'lar Jim Bean.'

The pair took hold of the glasses and each took a swig. They grinned. The whiskey was exactly what Earl Peplow had said it was.

'Thanks, Earl. This is damn good stuff!' declared Burke.

'Yeah. Wa'al, you said we got things to discuss, Jed,' remarked Peplow.

''Deed I did.'

'Go ahead, then. I'm a-listenin'.'

'Them youngsters we locked in your barn. You wanted us to shoot 'em.'

'That's so.'

'Why?'

'It's a long story.'

'We got time; ain't we, Bill?'

'Sure have,' concurred Hudson.

'But mebbe you don't need to know,' said Peplow.

'No?' said Burke.

'No. Let's say I pay you each a coupla hundred dollars an' you jest forgit you ever saw 'em?'

Burke and Hudson exchanged glances.

'You're gonna kill 'em, ain't you?' enquired Burke.

'If 'n' I don't tell you, an' you don't know, then you're both in the clear,' stated Peplow.

Again Burke and Hudson exchanged glances, but this time it was Bill Hudson who spoke.

'We ain't bein' a party to no killin',' he said flatly. 'It don't matter that you don't tell us. We brought 'em here, so we're involved whether we like it or not.'

'Yeah. An' a measly four hundred dollars ain't enough to buy our silence,' rasped Burke.

'I see.' Peplow smiled coldly. Four hundred bucks could in no way be termed measly, not by someone as strapped for cash as was Jed Burke. He and Hudson were, like Peplow himself, barely scratching a living on their farm. It was evident, therefore, that Burke suspected there was a deal more money to be had. 'You really wanta know the whole story, huh?' he asked.

'We do. Otherwise we free them kids,' said Burke.

'OK. I give in.' Peplow had no option. He had neither the time nor the imagination to think up a lie. 'You know Cousin Nathan was proposin' to marry the Widder Morgan?' he said.

'Yeah,' replied Burke.

'Wa'al, he told me they planned to tie the knot jest as soon as he got back from his business trip to Mustang Pass.

Imagine that!' Peplow took a sip of whiskey and continued, 'Jane Morgan, she's pretty goddam wealthy already. She don't need Nathan's money, but I do. Hell, if they married an' he went an' died, she'd inherit! I'd git nothin'.'

'What . . . what are yuh sayin' Earl?' gasped Burke.

'I'm sayin' I followed Nathan to Mustang Pass an' shot him dead.'

'But I thought it was some thief who . . .'

'That's what everyone thinks. An' that's the way it's gonna stay.'

'Y . . . yeah. You can rely on us to keep our mouths shut,' said Hudson, adding with a grin, 'For a consideration, of course.'

'Of course.' Peplow laughed harshly and stated, 'But you'll git nothin' if I'm arrested an' convicted of Nathan's murder.'

'There ain't no likelihood of that, surely?' remarked Hudson.

'There is while them two youngsters live,' replied Peplow.

'Whaddya mean?'

'I mean, Bill, that they witnessed the killin'. The girl could identify me for sure. I believe, though I ain't certain, that the boy could, too.'

'Holy cow!' exclaimed Jed Burke.

'Do they know you're here in Miller County?' enquired Bill Hudson.

'Oh, yeah! They spotted me. Which is why I had to stop 'em reachin' the Big Canyon. If 'n' they'd reached it an' blurted out their story to their uncle, Henry Turpin, then . . . '

'How'd you know they were Henry Turpin's nephew an' niece?' growled Hudson.

'Wa'al, Henry's been on about 'em comin' for some days now. An', seein' as the nearest stagecoach stop is at Mustang Pass, I guess I put two an' two together. I assumed, since they was brother an' sister an' 'bout the right age, that they was Henry's young relations headin' north on their way up here to Miller County.'

'So, why didn't you bushwack 'em

'tween Mustang Pass an' here?' asked Burke.

'I tried. You remember those three desperadoes holed up here last week?'

'Oh, yeah; Sheriff Brand wasn't none too happy 'bout their presence in town.'

'That's right, Jed. Wa'al, I rode back here an' hired 'em to ambush the youngsters somewhere along the trail.'

'So, what happened?'

'Some goddam Kentuckian gunfighter, name of Stone, happened along an' gunned down all three.'

'Jeeze!' cried Burke.

'So, I got Wally an' Willy Gregg to try an' pick 'em off after they arrived in Boulder Creek. Seems they decided to go for the boy first, an' once again that feller Stone intervened. This time he shot both Wally an' Willy.'

'Wow! He must be quite some shootist!' exclaimed Hudson.

'He is. A one-time lawman. Fortunately, it was assumed that he, an' not the youngsters, was the target. It appears that some time back he shot the brother of one of the desperadoes.'

'That might explain the ambush on the trail, but it don't explain why the Gregg brothers tried to kill him,' commented Hudson.

'No, it don't. Anyways, if 'n' the law, in the person of Joe Brand, thinks that's the case, wa'al, it's OK by me.'

'I s'pose it is. But, if the youngsters fail to arrive at the Big Canyon, ain't that gonna be a mite suspicious?' said Burke.

'Yeah. Mebbe Joe'll have second thoughts, start investigatin'?' suggested Hudson.

'Joe Brand likes a quiet life. He ain't gonna stir hisself. No doubt Henry Turpin will git his men to scour the terrain hereabouts, but he won't find nothin'. And so, in due time, the fuss will die down an' their disappearance, while remainin' a mystery, will be forgotten.'

'Hmm. You think so?' Jed Burke sounded doubtful.

'Whether it does or not, there will be

nothin' to link that disappearance with any of us.'

'No?'

'No, Jed.' Earl Peplow eyed both men keenly. 'Look, fellers,' he said, 'I was a li'l miserly jest now. How's about I cut you in for a thousand bucks each?'

'An' we forgit we ever saw 'em?' said Burke.

'That's right.'

'I still don't like it.'

'Me neither,' said Hudson. 'I don't wanta be no . . . what's the word? . . . accessory to murder.'

'That's a lotta money you're turnin' down.'

'I know.' Hudson bit his lip and cogitated for a few moments. 'How's about givin' us a li'l time to think it over? There ain't no tearin' hurry after all, for them youngsters ain't goin' nowhere,' he said.

'True,' replied Peplow.

He reckoned that, once the twins were dead, his neighbours would be accessories whether they wanted to be or not. They would be compromised and unable to betray him without taking the chance that they themselves could be tried and imprisoned, maybe even hanged. A plan began to form in his mind.

'Wa'al?' queried Burke.

'OK, fellers,' he said. 'I figure you're entitled to talk this whole thing over 'fore you come to a decision. An', while you're doin' that, I reckon I'll ride back into town an' have a word with Vernon Oakridge 'bout the readin' of the will. Plumb forgot to do that this mornin'. I don't s'pose I'll be back till mid-afternoon, by which time I hope you boys'll have reached some kinda con-clusion.'

'You . . . you aim to ride into town, leavin' them kids locked in your barn?' exclaimed Hudson.

In fact, a foray into town for a discussion with the lawyer was not what Peplow really had in mind. He intended to set out and then, once he was sure that Jed Burke and Bill Hudson had gone back to their own farm, he proposed to turn around and head for home. By the time they returned for their midafternoon powwow, he would have killed the twins and the two would be fatally compromised.

'Wa'al, I guess we'll ride in with you,' said Jed Burke.

'Jest to keep you company,' added Bill Hudson, with a wide grin.

Outwardly, Earl Peplow was smiling. Inwardly, he was cursing.

'But you must have work you could be gittin' on with on your farm!' he exclaimed.

'Nothin' that partickerly needs doin' this mornin'.'

'But, Bill . . . '

'We'll ride along,' Hudson reiterated.

'Yeah. 'Sides, I'm aimin' to sit in on the Sunday evenin' poker game like I usually do. It starts at six o'clock prompt,' added Burke.

'So, yo're proposin' to stay on in town?'

'That's right, Earl.'

'But what about that decision you need to make?'

'Me an' Bill can be thinkin' it over on the way into town an' while you're closeted with Mr Oakridge.'

'Yeah. An' we could mebbe drop into the Trail's End for a coupla beers,' added Hudson. 'Then, when your business is done, you could join us an' we could let you know what we've decided.'

'In the Trail's End! For Pete's sake! That's a darned sight too public!'

'No, it ain't. It'll be pretty quiet mid-afternoon. All we gotta do is find a corner table, well away from the bar, an' make sure we keep our voices down,' said Burke.

Earl Peplow scowled. It was clear that the other two had guessed what he had in mind and were determined to thwart him. The point was: what would their decision be? Peplow continued to scowl. He was stymied. All he could do was hope that their avarice would outweigh their fear of being found out and hanged.

'OK, fellers,' he said, 'we'll play it your way.'

The other two quickly mounted their horses and, keeping a sharp eye on the barn in which Ben and Laura were imprisoned, waited while Peplow reluctantly mounted his grey mare.

However, Earl Peplow had not yet admitted defeat. He tried one last time to dissuade his neighbours from joining him.

'You really sure you wanta come?' he asked. 'I mean, there ain't no need for you to set out this early, Jed, if 'n' your poker game don't commence till six o'clock.'

'We're comin',' stated Burke flatly.

'We sure are,' confirmed Hudson.

'OK. Let's be on our way,' said Peplow, bowing to the inevitable.

He set his mare in motion and, flanked by Burke and Hudson, cantered out of the farmyard and along the trail towards Boulder Creek.

They were two miles down the trail

when Jed Burke suddenly cursed and reined in his pinto. Both Peplow and Hudson promptly did likewise.

'What the hell?' demanded Earl Peplow.

'My specs! I forgot my specs!' exclaimed Burke.

'What in tarnation are you talkin' about?' rasped Peplow.

'Jed needs his specs for readin',' explained Hudson.

'So?'

'I'm gonna need 'em to play poker,' said Burke.

'Holy cow!'

'It's OK, Earl. You an' Bill ride on. I'll slip back an' git my specs, an' meet you at the Trail's End.'

Earl Peplow nodded. 'Right, Bill; let's git movin',' he said. Then, glancing at Burke, he growled 'See you later, Jed.'

'Yeah.'

Jed Burke straightaway turned the pinto's head and set off back in the direction of the two farms.

Ben and Laura Johnson had protested loudly when Jed Burke and Bill Hudson shut them in Earl Peplow's barn. But to no avail.

They had continued to shout as the barn door was barred and locked. They had rattled it and pushed against it without success. It had not budged.

'What's goin' on?' sighed Laura. 'Why did those men lock us in here?'

'Cain't you guess?' asked Ben.

'That man who murdered the mayor!' cried Laura.

'Yup. I reckon he sent those two varmints after us.'

'With instructions to lock us in this here barn?'

'Guess so.'

'What . . . what do you think he's gonna do to us, Ben?'

'He cain't afford to let us live.'

'Wa'al, why didn't his two confederates jest shoot us, if that's who they are?'

'Dunno, Laura. Mebbe they prefer to leave the killin' to him?'

'Yes, mebbe.'

'So, Laura, we gotta git outa here 'fore he turns up.'

'I wonder why he didn't pursue us hisself?'

'Your guess is as good as mine. But let's not worry 'bout that. Let's see if we can find any way outa this here barn.'

'OK.'

They looked round the dim interior. Although there were no windows, some light filtered through the narrow gaps between the planks that formed its walls. Also, there was a small, jagged hole in the roof. There was no way, however, that they could reach this hole and clamber through it to freedom.

Several bales of straw were stacked against one wall, while a number of empty wooden boxes and barrels stood singly and in piles at the far end of the barn.

It was while he was searching idly

through these that Ben chanced upon the discarded and broken hoe.

'Wow!' he cried.

'What have you found? Oh, is that all?' demanded Laura disappointedly, on observing the hoe.

'This is gonna git us outa here,' replied Ben.

'How?'

'The walls of this barn consist of 'bout a dozen staves driven into the ground at intervals, with planks nailed onto them. Right?'

'Right.'

'Wa'al, beneath the bottommost plank there's only earth. So, all I gotta do is dig enough of that earth away to enable us to crawl out.'

'Gee, Ben, do you reckon you can do that?'

'I do. Let's jest hope I can do it 'fore that killer turns up.'

'Oh, yes, indeed!'

Ben immediately dropped onto his knees and began digging away beneath the rear wall of the barn, next to one of the stacks of wooden boxes. He chose this wall to dig under since he had no idea whether Peplow's confederates remained in the vicinity. If they did, he thought it likely they would be keeping an eye on the front of the barn. He hoped, therefore, that his digging at the rear would pass unnoticed.

Digging a hole big enough for him and his sister to pass through was not easy, particularly with only a broken hoe for a tool. The earth was hard-baked and, even with a spade, he would have found it extremely difficult to dig. Nevertheless, he persevered, blistering and bloodying his hands in the process.

★   ★   ★

The minutes passed into hours, the morning progressed. Earl Peplow returned from town. He had his confrontation with Jed Burke and Bill Hudson. They, all three, set out together for town. Then, not long after they had disappeared down the trail, Ben finally threw down the hoe and exclaimed:

'I've done it, Laura! I reckon that there hole's big enough for us to squeeze through.'

'What . . . what about those two men who locked us up in here?' cried the girl.

'They cain't possibly watch all four sides of the barn at once. An' it don't seem they've spotted me diggin' this hole.'

'No.'

'So, let's give it a go.'

'OK, but you go first.'

'Right.'

Ben got down onto his hands and knees, then dropped onto his belly and began to crawl into the hole. It was a tight squeeze. He could feel the bottom plank scraping his back as he wriggled beneath it. But eventually he emerged, dusty and exhausted, outside the barn. He looked carefully about him.

'Come on, sis! The coast's clear,' he whispered.

Laura mustered all her courage and dived head first into the hole. Being slightly slimmer than her brother, she passed through without any great difficulty. As she emerged into the sunshine, Ben stooped down and helped her onto her feet.

'Thank you, Ben. I . . . Oh, my God! Look!'

The girl, wide-eyed and ashen-faced, pointed. Ben whirled round to see Jed Burke bearing down on them.

'Quick! Follow me!' cried Ben.

He grabbed his sister's hand and set off in the direction of the farmhouse. He had observed earlier that his and his sister's horses were hitched to a rail in front of the porch. They reached the porch, but the horses were no longer there. Ben glanced anxiously about him. Jed Burke was now only a few yards away and closing. Also, he had drawn his Colt Peacemaker and was yelling at the two youngsters to stand still and stick their hands in the air.

'Oh, Ben, what are we gonna do?' wailed Laura.

'Inside!' hissed Ben.

He threw open the farmhouse door and dragged Laura into its dim and dusty interior. Then he slammed the door shut behind him.

'What now?' she cried.

'I dunno. I . . . ' Ben paused, as his eye suddenly alighted upon the twin-barrelled scattergun resting on a couple of pegs driven into the wall behind him. He crossed the room in half a dozen quick strides and snatched the shotgun off its two pegs. 'Step to one side, Laura,' he rasped.

The girl did as she was bid and seconds later the door was thrown open to reveal the sturdy, tough-looking Jed Burke, his eyes glinting malevolently and his revolver clutched in his right hand.

'Got you!' he chortled gleefully.

'Oh, no, you ain't!' retorted Ben, bringing up the scattergun and pointing it directly at the homesteader's chest.

The gun was cocked on both hammers and consequently, when Ben fired, the two barrels blasted a wide-spreading diamond pattern of ten-gauge shot straight at Jed Burke. The buckshot hit him full in the chest and knocked him clean through the open doorway, to land with a bone-shattering thud on the wooden porch outside.

There he lay, temporarily stunned and with blood oozing from a variety of buckshot wounds across the length and breadth of his upper body.

Clutching the scattergun with one hand and his sister with the other, Ben dashed out of the farmhouse and, skirting the fallen man, leapt off the porch and headed for the nearby hills. Not realizing that Peplow and Hudson were still on their way to town and fearing that one or other might appear at any moment, he did not attempt to find his and his sister's horses. Panic had taken hold of his senses and all he wanted to do was put as much distance as possible between himself and his murderous enemies.

'Where . . . where are we goin'?' enquired Laura, as they ran pell-mell through the sagebrush in the direction of the hills.

'I dunno,' he replied. 'I jest want us to git clear of here 'fore the mayor's killer an' that other feller turn up.'

Laura didn't argue. She was as anxious as her brother to stay well clear of the man she had observed in Nathan B. Marston's room in Mustang Pass's Grand Hotel, the man who had coldbloodedly murdered both the mayor and his sporting woman.

Jed Burke, meantime, was sitting up and taking notice. Although bleeding profusely, he was in no imminent danger of dying. He badly needed patching up and was still very shaken. But he would survive. He staggered to his feet, cursing beneath his breath. Any compunction he might have had about killing the two youngsters had been dispelled by that blast of buckshot.

There was murder in his heart as he slowly and painfully remounted the pinto.

Digging his heels into the horse's flanks, Burke set off once more towards Boulder Creek. He needed to have his wounds tended and, at the same time, he wanted to alert Peplow and Hudson regarding the twins' escape. He did not return to his own farmhouse to pick up the forgotten spectacles. Poker was no longer on his agenda.

# 7

Sheriff Joe Brand stood in the doorway of the law office and viewed the practically deserted Main Street. It was past noon and, the church service having ended some time earlier, most folk were by now at home preparing to enjoy their Sunday lunch. Joe Brand had attended the service and then proceeded to the law office to give Deputy Tim Hollis his instructions. Now he proposed to head for the Grizzly Bear, where he habitually had Sunday lunch with John Gordon and his family.

Brand was about to leave the stoop in front of the law office and cross the street to the hotel when he spotted Earl Peplow and Bill Hudson riding into town.

'Howdy, Earl. You back so soon? Hell, you ain't been gone above an hour!' he exclaimed.

'I need a word with Vernon Oakridge,' replied Peplow.

'Oh, yeah?'

'Yeah. 'Bout the readin' of the will, that kinda thing.'

''Course. You bein' Nathan's only kin, guess you're gonna be a pretty rich man.'

'I s'pose.'

Earl Peplow cantered on, closely followed by Bill Hudson. The sheriff watched them halt before the Trail's End saloon and dismount. He eyed Nathan B. Marston's heir speculatively as he disappeared through the batwing doors. In common with Jack Stone and most lawmen, Brand had a nose for pending trouble. This was why he had wanted the Kentuckian out of town, for he sensed that Stone was a man who, while he might not court it, nevertheless attracted trouble. And now his nose told him that something was not quite right. It was pure instinct. He had no real reason to suspect Peplow of anything untoward, yet he felt convinced that the homesteader had some guilty secret. He intended, therefore, to watch events very closely over the next day or so. In the meantime, he continued on his way across the street towards the Grizzly Bear hotel and lunch.

As he did so, Earl Peplow and Bill Hudson reached the bar counter, where Peplow ordered a couple of beers.

'What about Jed?' enquired Hudson.

'We don't know how long he's likely to be,' replied Peplow.

'He shouldn't be very long.'

'Depends on if he can find them specs. If he's mislaid 'em an has to go lookin' for 'em, wa'al . . . ' Peplow shrugged his shoulders.

'Yeah, that's true,' agreed Hudson.

'So, let's take these beers over to that table in the corner,' suggested Peplow.

They proceeded to the table indicated by Earl Peplow and sat down. Then, when they had both enjoyed a good swig of the beer, Peplow said quietly:

'There ain't no alternative, you know. Them youngsters gotta die. If 'n' they don't, they'll spill the beans an' I'll hang for sure.'

'I s'pose so.'

'In which case, you an' Jed'll git nothin'.'

'Wa'al . . . '

'I need 'em dead. We all three need 'em dead.'

'I still don't like . . . '

'Come on, Bill, we ain't got no choice. I don't partickerly wanta kill 'em, but I'm afraid I must.'

'I . . . I still gotta talk it over with Jed.'

'If an' when he gits here.'

'Yeah. Anyways, I thought you was intendin' payin' Vernon Oakridge a visit?'

'I am, but it's lunchtime. I should've thought of that 'fore we set out. Guess I'll have me a few beers first.'

'I see.' Bill Hudson frowned. The

mention of lunchtime reminded him that he had not eaten since very early that morning.

'Wa'al, I reckon, when Jed turns up, him an' me'll mosey on over to Mexican Pete's an' grab us somethin' to eat. We can talk things over there while we dine.'

'Providin' you keep your voices down.'

'We ain't stupid.' Hudson looked decidedly nettled.

'No, no; I didn't mean to imply you was,' replied Peplow hastily.

Thereafter, the two men lapsed into a gloomy silence. Then, when they had finished their beers, Peplow, anxious to placate the other, went up to the bar and fetched two more.

It was as they were finishing this second round that the batwing doors were pushed open and the bloodied figure of Jed Burke staggered into the saloon. He immediately spotted them and tottered across the bar-room towards their table.

The Sunday morning poker-game had finished and the players had all dispersed to their homes for lunch. Therefore, apart from Peplow and Hudson, only a couple of drinkers at the bar and the bartender remained. The drinkers had their backs to Burke as he came in, while the bartender had seen it all before and was not in the least concerned at the sight of Burke's blood-splattered appearance. He simply continued to polish the beer-glass in his hand, without so much as batting an eyelid.

'What in tarnation's happened to you?' demanded Earl Peplow as the wounded man slumped onto a chair.

'Whaddya goddam think?' exclaimed Burke. 'I got shot, that's what.'

'I can see that,' retorted Peplow. 'The point is, how did you git shot an' who did it?'

'Henry Turpin's nephew; that's who!'

'All right! All right! Keep your voice down, darn it!' Peplow laid a hand on the other's shoulder. 'Jest tell us what happened, Jed,' he murmured.

'He an' his sister escaped from your barn. Dug their way out.'

'No!'

'Sure did. I gave chase an' they ran into your farmhouse.'

'So, you had 'em cornered.'

'Yup. Only the boy, he grabbed your scattergun off the wall an' blasted me with it.'

'Jeeze!'

'A pepperin' of buckshot ain't likely to prove lethal, but it sure as hell hurts! 'Sides, I lost a considerable quantity of blood. Reckon I need patchin' up pretty damn quick.'

'OK, Jed; I'll go fetch Doc Harris,' volunteered Bill Hudson.

'You do that,' concurred Peplow. 'I'll take care of Jed till you git back.'

'Right.'

Peplow turned back to Burke and said quietly. 'You sit tight. I'll go git the whiskey bottle an' a coupla glasses.'

'Make that three glasses.'

Peplow whirled round to discover that the speaker was none other than Sheriff Joe Brand.

'Oh, hi there, Joe!' he muttered.

'Jed looks to be in a bad way,' commented the sheriff.

'I'll survive,' remarked Burke.

'Buckshot,' explained Peplow.

'How come?' enquired Brand.

'Er . . . Jed was jest explainin'. Chanced to be passin' my farm an' spotted an intruder. Chased the feller into my farmhouse. Only the feller grabbed my shotgun off the wall an' blasted Jed with it.'

'You want I should ride out there?' enquired Brand.

'No, that's OK, Joe. Bill's gone to git hold of Doc Harris. Soon as the doc arrives, me an' Bill will go searchin' for the varmint.'

'Wa'al, I'm the law round here . . . '

'You've got enough to do without chasin' off out into the hills after some pesky sneak-thief. We know the territory pretty good. We'll git him,

131

don't you worry.'

'If 'n' you're sure?'

'I'm sure.'

Brand nodded. He had been sitting by one of the windows in the Grizzly Bear and had spotted Jed Burke ride into town. Naturally, as the upholder of law and order in Miller County, he had straightaway risen from the lunch table and dashed after the stricken home-steader.

Now, observing the man's blood-stained state, he wondered idly if the story spun by Earl Peplow was true. There was no reason to doubt it, yet his instincts once again told him that something didn't quite ring true. He continued to study the wounded man while Peplow fetched the whiskey and the three glasses.

'Are you certain we ain't keepin' you, Joe?' enquired Peplow, as he placed the glasses on the table and proceeded to fill them from the bottle.

'No; I jest 'bout finished lunch,' replied the sheriff. He lifted one of the glasses. 'To your speedy recovery, Jed,' he said.

'Thanks.'

Jed Burke threw back his whiskey at one gulp and, not waiting for Peplow to do the honours, promptly refilled the glass himself. He tossed back this second whiskey and then proceeded to pour a third.

'I sure as hell needed them slugs of whiskey!' he declared solemnly.

As he spoke, Bill Hudson came hurrying into the saloon with Doc Harris in tow.

The doctor, a small, bespectacled, serious-faced man in his late fifties, viewed Jed Burke with a cool, professional eye.

'Wa'al, wa'al, wa'al!' he drawled. 'You're in one helluva mess, Jed.'

'I don't need tellin' that. I already know,' rasped Burke.

'No need to be so tetchy,' responded the doctor. He eyed the other's badly bloodstained shirt. 'Guess I'll need to cut you outa that,' he said. 'Then I can set about diggin' out them shotgun pellets. After which I'll patch you up.'

'Thanks, Doc,' said Burke, in a distinctly unenthusiastic tone.

If he was less than happy at the prospect of enduring what he assumed would be a particularly painful operation, Earl Peplow and Bill Hudson were no keener on observing it. He had no choice in the matter, however, whereas they most decidedly had.

'We'll leave you to it, then,' said Peplow.

'What! You're gonna abandon me?' cried Burke.

'Me an' Bill gotta git after that varmint who shot you. Ain't that so, Bill?' remarked Peplow.

'Yup,' said Hudson.

'But . . . '

'We'll see you back at my place,' said Peplow. 'Once the doc's patched you up an' you feel fit enough, jest ride on back there, OK?'

'OK,' grunted Burke.

'One thing before we go, though.'

'Yeah?'

'Did . . . did this er . . . thief steal a hoss or . . . ?'

'No. They . . . I mean, he . . . made off on foot.'

'In which direction?'

'I . . . I didn't see. By the time I crawled outa your farmhouse they . . . er . . . he had vanished. My guess is he headed into the hills to the south of your farm, them bein' the nearest.'

'OK. Thanks, Jed.'

'You . . . you be sure an' kill the li'l bastard!' hissed Burke.

Peplow smiled grimly. The shotgun blast had evidently helped change Burke's mind. Now all he, Peplow, had to do was convince Hudson.

'I'll do my darnedest,' he promised.

# 8

In the heart of the hills to the south of Earl Peplow's farm was a narrow gulch through which flowed a clear, fast-running stream. It was in the shelter of a tumble of boulders and close by this stream that Ben and Laura Johnson had holed up. They had slept fitfully and were wide awake at first light.

Ben rose and looked about him. He still clutched the shotgun he had taken from Earl Peplow's farmhouse. Why he had hung onto it, he could not think, for it was empty and he had no ammunition with which to reload it. He had carried it instinctively, much as he had run off into the hills with but one aim in mind, to escape from his captors.

Ben reckoned that it was extremely unlikely that Nathan B. Marston's killer and his confederates would track him and his sister to their hiding-place. However, he also realized that he and Laura could not remain there forever. They had water but no food, and he was already very hungry.

'We gotta git outa here, sis,' he informed the girl.

'Yes.' Laura rose and stretched. 'But where do we head for?'

'Wa'al, I'd like to head for the Big Canyon ranch, only I ain't sure whereabouts that lies from here.'

'No.'

'I figure we're 'bout four or five miles south of that farm where we were locked up. Do you agree?'

'I s'pose.'

'So, if we wend our way through these hills in a westerly direction, we should come outa them somewhere near Boulder Creek.'

'Is that what you think we should do, head back to town?'

'Yup. I don't see that we have any alternative.' Ben sighed and said contritely, 'Mebbe we should've stayed in town an' gone lookin' for the sheriff like you suggested. Then we wouldn't be in this mess. I'm so sorry, Laura.'

'No; you did what you thought was for the best. An', if we'd stayed in town, those two fellers who rode after us might've caught us anyway. I mean, we didn't know that the sheriff was at the law office. He could've been out on his rounds, or at church, or some place else.'

'That's possible, I grant you. Nevertheless, I feel I made the wrong decision. We should've stayed in town.'

'Wa'al, that's in the past. What's done is done. So, let's forget it an' do as you say, head westward through these hills an' hope to find Boulder Creek on their far side. How far off do you reckon it is from here?'

'Dunno? 'Bout seven or eight miles, mebbe? It's difficult to judge, for we ain't gonna be able to go exactly in a straight line.'

'I guess not.'

'I jest wish we had our hosses.'

'Never mind, Ben; if we stride out, we should git there by mid-mornin'. Then our troubles'll be over.'

'That's the spirit, sis!' Ben, cheered by his sister's optimism, took her by the hand and, setting off up the gulch, declared, 'We'll make it! 'Course we will!'

It took some little time to emerge from the gulch, whereupon they were faced with a pretty tough scramble up a steep hillside. Both youngsters were hot and sweating and breathing heavily by the time they reached the summit. Their calves and thighs ached abominably for neither was used to hill-climbing. They looked around them and noted thankfully that a narrow ridge ran between the summit of the hill they had just climbed and the next two immediately to the west of it. This meant that they could head in approximately the direction they wished to go without descending and ascending these hills. They could simply follow the ridge.

Once they had recovered their breath, the twins strode off along this ridge, keeping an eye open for any sight of their enemies, who they assumed would be out looking for them.

Ben and Laura were correct in this assumption. While Earl Peplow headed for town to attend his cousin's funeral, Bill Hudson and Jed Burke resumed the search for the youngsters. Burke, having been patched up by Doc Harris and having exchanged his blood-splattered, pellet-ridden shirt for a fresh one, was as keen as Peplow to kill the twins. He was thirsting for vengeance. Hudson, on the other hand, was still a rather reluctant accomplice. He badly wanted the promised $1,000, yet he had reservations about involving himself in murder.

The two searchers split up, Jed Burke riding eastward through the hills towards the prairie, while Bill Hudson rode westward in the general direction of Boulder Creek. So it was that, upon reaching the summit of the third hill and observing the town no more than two miles off to the south-west, Ben and Laura spotted Hudson riding a winding trail between the hills, a trail they must cross. They promptly dropped out of sight behind a large boulder.

'What now?' cried Laura. 'That . . . that's one of them, an' he's sure to catch us if we try to outrun him, him bein' on hossback an' us on foot.'

'Yeah.' Ben mused upon this problem for some moments, all the while watching Hudson canter towards them along the trail. 'He's on his own,' he said at last.

'So?'

'So, Laura, we outnumber him two to one.'

'But he's armed.'

'So am I.'

'No, you're not. That shotgun ain't loaded. 'Deed, I dunno why you've held onto it.'

'I'm not sure why either,' confessed

Ben. 'However, mebbe it's as well I have.'

'Whaddya mean?'

'I mean, Laura, that it could save our lives.'

'How on earth . . . ?'

'That feller who's pursuin' us don't know it ain't loaded.'

'No,' Laura stared speculatively at her twin brother. 'What plan have you in mind?' she asked.

Ben quickly explained. Then, when he had finished, he enquired, 'Are you game, sis?'

The girl nodded.

'It . . . it could jest work,' she remarked brightly.

'It will work!' declared Ben.

So saying, he rose cautiously to his feet and began to scramble down the far side of the hill. This rendered him out of sight of Bill Hudson, yet took him directly down to the trail along which the homesteader was cantering. Laura followed, slipping and slithering on the patches of scree and grabbing hold of the occasional sagebrush to prevent her from tumbling all the way down the steep hillside.

In this manner the youngsters made their descent and eventually reached the trail below, whereupon Ben carefully studied the surrounding area. To his left, the trail ran in a straight line to join the main trail into town. To his right was a sharp bend with an overhang. Ben bent down and picked up a large rock. He handed this to Laura and pointed to the overhang.

'You know what to do, sis,' he said quietly.

The girl nodded and headed towards the overhang. She then climbed back up the hillside a few yards until she was level with the flat summit of the overhang. She stepped onto this summit and remained crouching there while Ben walked down the trail and halted beneath the rocky protrusion. Both waited, listening intently to the sound of the approaching hoofs.

Presently Bill Hudson cantered

round the bend in the trail and, upon spying Ben Johnson standing there in front of him and pointing Earl Peplow's scattergun at him, straightaway reined in his horse.

'Whoah!' he cried.

'You lookin' for me?' demanded Ben.

'You . . . you be careful with that there gun. It . . . it could go off!' exclaimed a suddenly nervous Bill Hudson.

'I asked you a question,' said Ben.

'Yeah, wa'al . . . er . . . mebbe I am an' mebbe I ain't,' muttered Hudson, not quite knowing what to say and, at the same time, calculating whether he could draw and shoot his revolver before the youngster squeezed the trigger.

He noted that the shotgun appeared to be cocked on both hammers. This was not good news, particularly as Hudson was by no means the fastest gun in the West. He suspected, though, that the gun might not be loaded. It was undoubtedly the same weapon which had blasted Jed Burke. And, from what Burke had said, it seemed unlikely that the youngster could have reloaded it. But of this Hudson could not be certain.

Hudson was still debating whether or not to go for his gun when Laura leapt up and tiptoed across the flat summit of the rocky outcrop until she was stationed directly above the home-steader. Thereupon, she raised the rock above her head and hurled it down-wards with all the force she could muster. It struck Hudson on the top of the head, crushing his Stetson and knocking him out of the saddle. He hit the dusty trail with a sickening thud and lay quite still. Laura gazed down at his spread-eagled body and gasped.

'Have . . . have I killed him?' she cried.

'I dunno,' replied Ben. 'An' I don't care. One thing is for sure, he's out cold. So, git down here as quick as you can!'

Laura needed no second bidding.

She hurriedly scrambled down the hillside to join her brother on the trail. He, meantime, had grabbed hold of Bill Hudson's horse, which had wandered off.

'OK, Laura, let's git the hell outa here!' he cried, as he climbed into the saddle.

'Right.'

Laura stretched up and took hold of Ben's hand. Straightaway, he hoisted her up behind him. Then, he dug his heels into the horse's flanks and set off down the trail in the direction of Boulder Creek.

Behind them, Bill Hudson stirred slightly, Laura had not, as she suspected, killed him. His thick skull had saved him. Yet it was some minutes before he recovered sufficiently to sit up. He had a lump the size of an egg on the top of his head and it ached unmercifully. He closed his eyes and sat there for half an hour or more, quite unable to move, so concussed was he.

Finally, painfully and unsteadily,

Hudson rose to his feet. Indeed, so painful was his skull that he could not bear to replace his Stetson. Instead, he carried the hat in his hand. His mind was in a whirl, he did not know what to do. Should he head for town or return to Earl Peplow's farmhouse? He imagined that the youngsters would be in Boulder Creek by now, spilling the beans. In which case, Peplow was likely to swing and he and Jed Burke were both in big trouble. Perhaps he should make a run for it? But where would he go? And how far would he get on foot? Hudson decided that Peplow's farmhouse was about as far as he could manage. Once there, maybe he could rest up for a little while and review the situation. Slowly, shakily, he staggered off, back the way he had come.

While Bill Hudson was still coming to his senses, Ben and Laura Johnson were riding into town. They found Main Street to be completely deserted, since the entire population was attending Nathan B. Marston's funeral. They clattered down the street, watching out for the law office. Then, having found it, Ben reined in their horse and they dismounted. Ben hitched the horse to the rail outside, and they climbed up the steps onto the stoop and went inside.

The law office, too, was deserted. Sheriff Joe Brand and his deputy, Tim Hollis, were, like everybody else, attending the funeral.

Ben and Laura settled down to wait. Anxious to tell their tale to the sheriff, they found the wait interminable. In fact, though, it was no more than twenty minutes before Sheriff Joe Brand came marching in. He was alone, Tim Hollis having remained behind to say a few consoling words to the Widow Morgan, who happened to be his aunt.

'Who the . . . ?' Brand started at the sight of the two youngsters. Then, he suddenly recognized Ben and Laura and smiled. 'You're Henry Turpin's nephew an' niece! Hell, your uncle's been lookin' everywhere for you! Didn't you follow that map I drew for you?' he demanded.

'We followed it,' said Ben.

'Wa'al, then, how in tarnation did you git lost?'

'We didn't.'

'But . . . '

'We were kidnapped.'

'Kidnapped!'

'Yes.'

'Why in blue blazes would anyone wanta kidnap you an' your sister?'

'In order to kill us.'

'Jeeze!' Joe Brand retreated behind his desk and sat down heavily. 'You'd best tell me the whole story,' he said.

'Yessir.'

Ben told the sheriff everything, beginning with the murder of the mayor in Mustang Pass's Grand Hotel and ending with the KO'ing of Ben Hudson two miles outside Boulder Creek. When he had finished, Joe Brand sat for some moments lost in thought.

'Is . . . is Ben's description of the mayor's murderer an' those two men who kidnapped us sufficient for you to identify them?' enquired Laura anxiously.

'Oh yes!' said Brand. 'I know exactly who they are.'

'So you'll arrest 'em?' said Ben.

'Naturally.' The sheriff stared thoughtfully at the twins and added, 'In the meantime, what am I gonna do 'bout you two?'

'Whaddya mean?' asked Ben.

'Wa'al, I'll need you both to make a formal identification so's I can arrest 'em an' throw 'em in jail.'

'We . . . we'll come with you, then,' volunteered Ben. 'Won't we, sis?'

'Oh . . . er . . . yes; we'll come with you,' Laura agreed nervously.

Joe Brand shook his head.

'No,' he said. 'I don't think that'd do at all. I figure it'll be much safer for you if 'n' I round 'em up an' bring 'em along here to the law office. Then you can identify 'em an' I'll formally charge 'em!'

'Wa'al . . . ' began Ben.

'You an' your sister can wait through there.' Brand pointed to the door leading through to the cells. 'I'll make sure all three are disarmed 'fore I call you out to look 'em over.'

Laura smiled faintly at her brother.

'That seems like a good idea, Ben,' she said.

'I s'pose,' said Ben.

'That's settled, then,' stated Brand.

'But how . . . how d'you propose to arrest all three of 'em? I mean, there's only one of you,' remarked Ben.

'I ain't gonna arrest 'em exactly,' explained the sheriff. 'I'm simply gonna ask 'em to accompany me to the law office to answer some questions. If 'n' they refuse, wa'al, I'll have Deputy Hollis with me to help persuade 'em.'

'I see.'

'Me an' the deppity are pretty darned quick with a gun, whereas the three fellers we're aimin' to pick up ain't.' Brand grinned. 'So, don't you worry, we'll bring 'em in,' he declared confidently.

He stepped across to the door leading to the cells and threw it open. Behind the door was a narrow passage facing onto three cells.

'You . . . you want us to stop in here?' said Ben.

'That's right. You'll be outa sight an' quite safe there.' Brand continued to grin. 'You can even choose your cell,' he added drily.

The two youngsters exchanged glances. Neither particularly wanted to spend time in one of the sheriff's cells, although each was provided with a reasonably comfortable-looking cot on which to sit or lie down.

'How . . . how long are you likely to be, Sheriff?' enquired Ben.

'Wa'al, it depends whether I find those varmints in town or have to mosey on out to their homestead. A coupla hours at most, I reckon,' said the lawman.

'OK,' said Ben.

He and his sister chose the middle cell and went in. Brand closed the door behind them, but did not lock it.

'I wouldn't've suggested this if there had been prisoners in the other cells,' he said.

'No,' said Ben.

'You two will be all right there?'

'Yes, Sheriff.'

'OK. I'll be as quick as I can.'

Joe Brand turned and re-entered the outer office, closing the connecting door behind him. As he did so, the lanky figure of Deputy Tim Hollis ambled into the law office.

'Ah, Tim!' cried Brand. 'I gotta job for you.'

'Oh, yeah?' said Hollis.

'Come outside. I'll explain as we go.'

'Go where, Sheriff?'

'Wa'al, I'm headin' for Vernon Oakridge's office,' replied Brand. He stepped outside and, quietly closing the law office door, turned to his young deputy and said, 'You recall I told you 'bout Jed Burke bein' shot by some goddam sneak-thief?'

'I surely do, Sheriff.'

'Wa'al, I got news a feller answerin' to this thief's description has been spotted in the vicinity of Coyote Wells.'

'Yeah?'

'Yeah; an' I want you to go investigate. The feller's 'bout six foot tall, big built an' with a bushy red beard. Dressed in a long brown leather coat an' brown derby hat, an' ridin' a piebald. You find him, you arrest him an' bring him back here to Boulder Creek.'

'But Coyote Wells is on the far side of the county! It'll take me till mid-afternoon 'fore I git there.'

'So?'

'Bringin' in a prisoner in daylight hours is one thing. Bringin' him in durin' the hours of darkness is another. That can be kinda tricky.'

'So, stick him in a cell in Coyote Wells overnight. Then bring him back here in the mornin'. 'Deed, if 'n' you don't find him, there ain't no need to ride back in the dark. You'd best stay till mornin', anyways.'

'What about my rounds?'

'I'll see to them.'

'Gee, thanks, Sheriff!'

Brand smiled. He knew that Tim Hollis had a sweetheart over in Coyote Wells and, consequently, would welcome the opportunity to spend the night there.

'You git goin' then, Tim.'

'Yessiree!'

The young deputy promptly mounted his horse, which was hitched to the rail outside, and headed off down Main Street at a gallop. Sheriff Joe Brand watched him go and then turned his steps in the direction of the lawyer's office.

Upon reaching it, however, he did not go inside. Instead, he sat himself down on the rocking-chair which Vernon Oakridge kept outside on the stoop. Then he lit a cheroot and patiently waited.

Half an hour passed before the door to the lawyer's office opened and Earl Peplow stepped outside. Brand promptly rose and greeted the home-steader.

'Howdy, Earl.'

'Oh . . . er . . . howdy, Joe!' Peplow replied, surprised by the sudden appearance of the sheriff, whom he had not noticed sitting in the rocking-chair.

'Has Vernon jest read the contents of Nathan's will?' enquired Brand.

'Yeah, that he has,' said Peplow smugly.

'You his sole heir, Earl?'

'I certainly am. I inherited everythin'. Wa'al, I am his only livin' kin after all.'

'Yeah. Congratulations.'

'Thanks, Joe.'

'Kinda lucky for you that Nathan died when he did, huh?'

'Whaddya mean?'

'I mean, he was set to marry Jane Morgan. 'Deed, rumour has it they was gonna fix a date as soon as he returned from that business trip to Mustang Pass.'

'So?'

'So, if he had returned, they'd've likely married an' then Jane Morgan would've been Nathan's next of kin.'

'I guess.'

'Lucky for you, then, that he never came back from Mustang Pass.'

'I . . . I didn't wish him dead, Joe. Hell, he was my cousin!'

'Yeah. Let's walk, Earl. I got somethin' to show you back at my office.'

'OK.'

The sheriff chose to walk not on the sidewalk, but down the middle of Main Street, which, at that hour, remained pretty well deserted.

'I guess we can talk freely here,' he said. 'So long as we keep our voices down, nobody's likely to overhear what we say.'

'An' why should I care if they do?' demanded Peplow.

'Because, Earl, I wanta talk about Nathan's murder.'

'I . . . er . . . I don't understand.'

'I think you do, Earl.'

'Jest what in blue blazes are you drivin' at?'

'Henry Turpin's niece witnessed that murder. She saw the murderer face to face an', when she arrived here in Boulder Creek yesterday, she spotted him again. Unfortunately, he also spotted her an' took steps to prevent her denouncin' him.'

'What . . . what are you sayin', Joe?'

'I'm sayin' you're that murderer, Earl.'

'No; I swear — '

'I got both Henry Turpin's niece an' his nephew back in the office.' Joe Brand grinned. 'They told me everythin'.'

'It . . . it's their word against mine.'

'An' who d'you think a jury will believe?'

'You . . . you ain't gonna arrest me, are you, Joe?'

As he spoke, Earl Peplow's hand dropped onto the butt of his Colt Peacemaker. Joe Brand, still grinning, shook his head.

'Take your hand off that gun. You know you ain't never gonna outdraw me,' he said.

Peplow slowly withdrew his hand.

'Wa'al?' he muttered.

'I ain't gonna arrest you,' said Brand. 'I'm gonna help you, but, if I do, I expect a share of your inheritance.'

'What have you in mind?'

'How much did you promise Jed an' Bill to kidnap them two youngsters?'

'One thousand dollars apiece.'

'OK. You pay 'em an' then everythin' else we split fifty-fifty.'

'But — '

'No buts, Earl. That's the deal. Take it or leave it.'

'OK. Only won't folks think it odd that I should split everythin' with you?'

'You'll explain that, unlike Nathan, you ain't much of a businessman, an' you wanted someone you could trust to help you run your cousin's businesses.'

'An' I figured you're that person?'

'Right, Earl.'

'Aw, OK!'

'I'll want this li'l arrangement made all nice 'n' legal. We'll git Vernon to draw up a contract.'

'When?'

'After we've disposed of Henry Turpin's niece an' nephew. But don't git no ideas 'bout double-crossin' me, Earl. I wouldn't like that.'

Earl Peplow stared into the sheriff's weasely face with its cold, pebble-black eyes. He concluded that it would be extremely unwise to attempt to play Joe Brand false. Half of Nathan B. Marston's estate would do very nicely. He could happily settle for that.

'There'll be no double-cross,' he promised. 'But firstly we gotta git rid of them pesky youngsters.'

'That's so.'

'You said they're in your office?'

'Yes. But nobody knows they're there. I've stuck 'em in the cells, so that anybody glancin' in through the office windows won't see 'em.'

'What about Tim, your deppity?'

'I've sent him across to the far side of the county, lookin' for the imaginary thief who peppered Jed with shotgun pellets. He won't be back till tomorrow mornin'.'

'That thief . . . ?'

'Was Henry Turpin's nephew.'

'Yup.'

'You sent Jed an' Bill out at first light, lookin' for them youngsters.'

'I did.'

'Wa'al, Bill found 'em. Only the girl dropped a rock on his head an' laid him low. Whether he's dead or merely KO'd, I couldn't say.'

'Holy cow!'

'Therefore, my plan is this: We go confront the youngsters, an' you help me tie 'em up an' gag 'em. Then, we leave 'em in the cell till after dark. 'Deed, I suggest till after midnight.'

'Oh, yeah?'

'Yeah. We don't want nobody to spot us when you take 'em outa my office an' off into the hills, where you're gonna kill 'em.'

'That'll be my pleasure,' said Peplow vindictively.

'An' we git Jed an' Bill, s'posin' Bill's still alive, to bury 'em,' concluded the sheriff.

'That's some plan!'

'You like it?'

'I surely do, Joe.'

'Then let's do it.'

As the sheriff spoke these words, they reached the law office. Leaving the dusty thoroughfare, the two men clambered up onto the stoop and stepped into the office. Here they paused to gather up the wherewithal to bind and gag their intended victims. Then, they pushed open the connecting door and marched through into the cells.

# 9

Henry Turpin mounted his black stallion and turned to face those gathered in front of his ranch house.

'OK, men,' he said, 'I want you to extend the range of your search. An' I want some of you to ride into the hills to the south of the Big Canyon. Mebbe the twins took the wrong fork 'fore they got this far. You organize things, Max.'

'Yessir,' said the foreman.

'I'll git back an' join you jest soon as I can. Gotta attend Nathan's funeral first,' said Turpin.

The rancher wanted desperately to ride out in search of his nephew and niece, and resented the fact that he could not do so immediately. However, punctilio dictated that he attend the mayor's funeral. He hoped, therefore, that it would not be a protracted affair.

'Mebbe we'll have found 'em by the

time you git back,' said Max Wayne.

'That'd be good,' stated Turpin.

Thereupon, he wheeled the stallion round and set off at a canter in the direction of Boulder Creek.

Max Wayne divided the search party into twos and once again Jack Stone was teamed with the young, red-headed cowhand, Buck Walters. They were among those dispatched to comb the hills to the south of the big Canyon ranch.

This they did diligently throughout the morning, neither stopping nor resting until the sun was high in the sky and they deemed it to be noon. Then they rode into the shade of a clump of cottonwoods and dismounted. Their fare was pretty simple: slabs of beef jerky and plain water from the water-bottles they carried.

Following this spartan meal, they sat awhile, smoking cheroots and talking.

'I guess life round here ain't usually this excitin'?' growled Stone.

'No, it ain't,' confirmed Buck Walters.

''Ceptin' Saturday nights at the Ace of Diamonds, it's pretty darned quiet.'

'But not since the murder of Boulder Creek's mayor down in Mustang Pass.'

'Nope. Since then, all hell's broke loose. There was that shoot-out 'tween you an' the Gregg brothers, an' then this mysterious disappearance of the boss's young nephew and niece.'

'There was also that ambush Saturday afternoon on the trail 'tween Mustang Pass an' Boulder Creek.'

'What ambush was that?' enquired the young cowboy.

'Three road agents jumped us . . .'

'Us?'

'Me an' the two youngsters. I figure they were after me, since one of 'em, Bobcat Deevers, held a grudge against me for shootin' his brother, Jethro, back in Dodge City. Though, how the hell he knew I was headin' this way, I cain't imagine.' Stone shrugged his shoulders and added, 'Mebbe he spotted me in Mustang Pass an' rode on ahead an' jest waited.'

'This Bobcat Deevers an' his two pals, can you describe 'em?' asked Buck Walters quietly.

'Sure,' said the Kentuckian. 'Deevers an' one of the others were both short, stocky, heavily bearded fellers, while the third varmint was tall an' thin. This taller feller had shoulder-length hair an' a kinda droopin' moustache, but no beard. All three wore brown derbies an' long brown leather coats.'

'Wa'al, I don't see how they could've been in Mustang Pass when you was there,' said Walters. 'Y'see, three fellers answerin' to that description was hangin' out in Boulder Creek till Saturday mornin'. I was in town pickin' up provisions when they rode out. They was headin' south.'

'If they were the same fellers.'

'I reckon they was. Rode into town a few days earlier an', so I was told, had been hangin' out at McBain's saloon ever since. Seems Sheriff Joe Brand was none too happy, but didn't wanta go up agin' 'em.'

'I see.'

The Kentuckian scratched his head thoughtfully. He needed to think and think hard.

'Buck,' he said, 'I got me some thinkin' to do. So, I figure I'll jest stay put awhile.

'You want me to stay with you?' asked the young cowboy. 'Or should I continue searchin' these here hills?'

'You carry on searchin'. Mebbe I'll catch you up an' mebbe I won't. If 'n' I don't, I'll likely meet up with you back at the Big Canyon.'

'OK, see you later.'

' 'Bye, Buck.'

Stone watched the cowboy mount his horse and head on out of the cottonwoods, before disappearing up a narrow gulch that wound its way southwards through the hills. He then lit a fresh cheroot and, with his back to a boulder, sat and mulled over the various events that had occurred since his meeting with Ben and Laura Johnson.

He had assumed that Bobcat Deevers and his pals had spotted him in Mustang Pass, guessed he was heading north and lain in wait for him. But, if they were in Boulder Creek while he was in Mustang Pass, then that was an impossibility. Also, why should the Gregg brothers, a couple of local ne'er-do-wells he had never met before, have wanted to kill him? It made no sense.

Stone drew hard on the cheroot and blew out a plume of smoke. There was, of course, another explanation, one which should have occurred to him earlier, namely that the target of both assassination attempts was not himself, but his travelling companions. He cursed himself for not having immediately hit upon what was, he now conceded, such an obvious explanation.

But why, he asked himself, would anybody want the two youngsters dead? Because they had witnessed the murder of Nathan B. Marston! And who would want them dead? The murderer, of course!

Stone smiled grimly. If he could find the mayor's killer, he felt sure that he would also find Ben and Laura Johnson. But would they be alive or dead, he wondered? Swiftly, he mounted his gelding and set off at a gallop after Buck Walters.

Half an hour later he caught up with the red-headed young ranch-hand.

'Mr Stone!' exclaimed Walters. 'I didn't expect to see you again this afternoon! You done thinkin'?'

'I have,' said Stone, as he rode alongside the cowboy. 'An' I need to know somethin',' he added firmly.

'Oh yeah?'

'Yeah, Buck. I need to know who stood to gain from the mayor's death.'

'You talkin' 'bout our mayor, ol' Nathan?'

'Who else?'

'Wa'al, his cousin's his sole heir, I guess.'

'His cousin?'

'Earl Peplow. Owns a homestead a

coupla miles south of the Big Canyon. Why are you askin'?'

'I think he may have murdered Mr Marston.'

'You crazy?'

'I don't think so. You wanta hear why I think he could be the mayor's killer?'

'Yeah. Tell me,' Buck Walters reined in his horse and immediately Jack Stone pulled up beside him. The cowboy looked rather sceptically at the Kentuckian and said, 'Go on, Mr Stone, I'm listenin'.'

'Wa'al, it's like this,' said Stone. 'Ben an' Laura Johnson were both in Mustang Pass the night Mr Marston was killed an', what's more, they witnessed the killin'. Now, the next day we was all three bush-whacked by three desperadoes on the trail 'tween there an' Boulder Creek. Then, once we reached Boulder Creek, an attempt was made on my life an' that of Ben Johnson at the Ace of Diamonds by a coupla local lunkheads. Now, suppose this Earl Peplow is Mr Marston's killer, wouldn't he want the witnesses to his crime silenced?'

'I . . . I guess so,' said Walters, his scepticism fading.

'Of course he would. So, what does he do? He heads back here an' hires Bobcat Deevers to ambush them. Only I happened along an' it was Bobcat an' his pals who died, not Ben and Laura.'

'Right.'

'Then, on hearin' that they'd arrived in Boulder Creek fit an' well, Earl Peplow promptly hired the Gregg brothers to do what Bobcat an' his pals had tried an' failed to do. But they decided to take Ben out first, which was lucky for Laura an' unlucky for them.'

'Gee!'

'It all ties up, Buck.'

'Assumin' that Earl was Nathan's killer, an' not some sneak-thief.'

'He had the motive.'

'Yeah. Nathan was a rich man, while Earl was strugglin' to make ends meet.'

'So, at least this Earl Peplow bears investigatin', don't you think?'

'Yes, Mr Stone, I do!' declared Walters, the last traces of scepticism banished.

'Then direct me to his homestead,' said the Kentuckian.

'You figure he may have Ben an' Laura confined somewhere thereabouts?'

'It's possible.'

'I'll guide you there.'

'OK, let's go.'

They wheeled their horses round and set off back in the direction from which they had come. The ride was a short one, of no more than a couple of miles. Then, all at once, the adjoining farms of Earl Peplow and his neighbours, Jed Burke and Bill Hudson, came into view in the valley below. Approaching Peplow's farm was a lone horseman.

'Is that him?' enquired Stone eagerly.

Buck Walters shook his head.

'Nope,' he said. 'That there is one of his neighbours, Bill Hudson.'

As the cowboy spoke, the door of

Earl Peplow's farmhouse suddenly opened and the farmer stepped outside. He beckoned to the approaching rider, who straightaway rode up to where Peplow was standing on the porch.

'Is that feller Earl Peplow?' demanded Stone.

'Yup; he surely is,' replied Walters.

'Then we'd best hang back,' said Stone, guiding his gelding into and behind a clump of sagebrush, which effectively hid him from the sight of the two homesteaders.

Buck Walters quickly joined him.

'Wa'al,' said Walters, 'what now?'

'I'm gonna nose around an' see what I can find out.'

'Shall I come with you?'

'Nope. You head on back to the Big Canyon an' await Mr Turpin's return. Tell him what I told you, an' say I'll report to him jest as soon as I succeed in locatin' his nephew an' niece.'

'D'you want him an' the boys to ride over an' . . . ?'

'Better not. We don't know for

certain that Ben an' Laura are here-abouts, an', if they ain't, it's mebbe best we don't let Earl Peplow know we're onto him.'

'So, how long do we wait for you to report?'

'For as long as it takes.'

'Mr Turpin ain't exactly the most patient of men.'

'You persuade him, Buck. One false move could easy jeopardize them youngsters' lives.'

'OK, Mr Stone, I'll do my darned-est,' promised Walters.

So saying, he stretched out and shook the Kentuckian's hand. Then, he cantered off, back in the direction of the Big Canyon. Jack Stone, meantime, dismounted and cautiously made his way downhill towards Earl Peplow's farm.

The Kentuckian dodged between clumps of mesquite, sagebrush and yucca as he proceeded down the hillside. He observed that the yard in front of the farmhouse was deserted except for Bill Hudson's horse, which stood hitched to the rail outside. Both Hudson and Earl Peplow had disappeared inside the house. From his vantage point behind a screen of sagebrush at the foot of the hillside, Stone carefully viewed the house. To reach it, he would need to dash across both the trail and the intervening yard. Should either of the farmhouse's inhabitants chance to glance out of the window, he would be seen for certain.

Stone decided, therefore, to work his way along the trail to a point mid-way between the two farms and cross the trail there. Then he could approach Peplow's farmhouse from the side, with much less likelihood of his being observed.

This he did, crossing the trail and then edging alongside the various outbuildings until he reached his objective. There was a small open window cut into the side wall of the farmhouse. Stone dared not peer in for fear of detection, but, from his position pressed close against the farmhouse wall, he could hear quite clearly every word spoken by those inside.

By the time Jack Stone had arrived beside the open window, Earl Peplow had produced a bowl of water and helped Bill Hudson bathe his bruised and bloodied head. He had also listened to Hudson's rather long-winded account of how he had been tricked and laid low by the two youngsters he was pursuing.

As Stone crouched beside the window, he heard Peplow growl angrily:

'You goddam lunkhead! You shoulda realized that shotgun the kid threatened you with was empty. Hell, he blasted Jed with it an' then straightaway took off into the hills! Where in blue blazes did you think he was gonna find the ammo to reload it? Under a Joshua tree, mebbe?'

'Wa'al, I . . . I didn't think it was loaded. Only I couldn't be sure an' so — ' began Hudson.

'Aw, never mind!' Peplow interrupted

him. 'Luckily, I found 'em.'

'You did!'

'Yeah.'

'Where . . . where are they?'

'In safe keepin'.'

'They . . . they ain't dead?'

'Nope.'

Outside, Stone breathed a sigh of relief and continued to listen intently.

'But you intend killin' them?'

'Yeah. You still opposed to the idea, Bill?'

'Not any more.' Hudson gingerly touched his tender scalp. 'I'll be more 'n pleased to oblige you there, Earl.'

'Wa'al, you won't have to. I'm gonna tend to that personally. What I'll need you an' Jed to do is bury their bodies.'

'For one thousand dollars each?'

'Yup. The price ain't changed. That OK by you?'

'It sure is, Earl. So, when do we do it? As soon as Jed gits back?'

'I don't s'pose he'll keep on lookin' for 'em after dark. I expect he'll mosey on back here somewhere about dusk.'

'I guess.'

'Wa'al, that's too darned early.'

'Whaddya mean? Why's it too early?'

''Cause I got 'em locked up in town an' I aim to take 'em outa town an' into the hills. That's where I plan to kill an' bury 'em.' Peplow grinned wickedly and said, 'I don't figure on movin' 'em till after midnight when Boulder Creek's main street is totally deserted.'

'Yeah; we certainly don't want anybody seein' us.'

'No.'

'So, where exactly have you got 'em locked up, Earl?'

Peplow continued to grin.

'I ain't sayin'. I wanta surprise you an' Jed.' He chuckled.

Stone cursed silently. Had Peplow divulged the place of Ben and Laura's confinement, he could have tried to release them while their three would-be killers were absent. Now he had no option other than to wait until the trio rode into town and follow them. In the meantime, he could, he supposed, ride over to the Big Canyon ranch and report to Henry Turpin. But he was loath to leave in case Earl Peplow changed his mind and acted earlier.

Not wishing to be spotted by the returning Jed Burke and needing to rejoin his gelding where he had left it, tethered in the midst of the sagebrush at the top of the hill opposite, Stone left the side of the farmhouse and retraced his steps. He moved with the same stealth that he had applied on the downhill journey. Past experience as an Army scout ensured that he covered the ground as silently as any light-footed Cheyenne. Then, upon reaching the clump of sagebrush at the summit, he lit a cheroot and settled down to wait.

# 10

It was ten minutes past midnight and Boulder Creek lay mostly in darkness. Only here and there did a shaft of yellow light spill out from some window or doorway. The Grizzly Bear hotel and McBain's saloon were both closed already, while the Trail's End was in the process of closing and the Ace of Diamonds had very few customers left. A typical Monday night.

The three riders trotted slowly down Main Street. Earl Peplow was flanked by Jed Burke and Bill Hudson, each of whom had a spade strapped to his saddle-boot. They reined in their horses in front of the law office, this being one of the few buildings still to be lit up. They dismounted, hitched their horses to the rail outside, climbed up onto the stoop and, pushing open the door, went inside.

As they disappeared from view a fourth rider pulled up his bay gelding some hundred yards or so away in the darkness of Main Street. He dismounted and hitched the gelding to a rail outside the town hall.

Thereupon, drawing his Frontier Model Colt from its holster, Jack Stone proceeded on foot towards the law office. He crept round to the back to find that the rear quarters, which included the cells, were, like the front office, all lit up. He peered through each of the three barred windows. However, since Ben and Laura lay bound and gagged on the cot immediately beneath the middle window, Stone failed to see them. Assuming the cells to be empty, he was about to make his way round to the front when, suddenly, the connecting door was flung open and Sheriff Joe Brand and his three visitors entered. Stone ducked down and, pressing close against the cell wall, listened intently.

'There you are, Earl,' said Brand,

pointing at the two prostrate figures on the cot in the middle cell.

Earl Peplow laughed harshly.

'Still hogtied, huh?' he said.

'Yeah. So don't forgit our deal,' rasped the sheriff.

'I won't, Joe,' promised Peplow.

'What deal would that be?' enquired Jed Burke.

'Like you an' Bill, Joe expects to be rewarded for his ... er ... co-operation.'

'How much is he gittin', then?' demanded Bill Hudson.

'That ain't none of your business, Bill,' said Brand. 'I ain't enquirin' into your an' Jed's deal. What's agreed 'tween me an' Earl is our concern.'

'That's right. An' you'll never earn an easier thousand bucks. All you gotta do is dig a li'l grave. Same applies to Jed,' said Peplow.

Jed Burke nodded.

'Yup. I ain't complainin'.'

'Nor me,' said Hudson hastily. Then, turning to the sheriff, he asked, 'You comin' out into the hills, Joe?'

'No. I've played my part,' said Brand.
'As for the rest, I'm leavin' it to Earl
to shoot 'em an' you an' Jed to bury
'em.'

'Oh! I thought you'd be comin' with
us,' said Peplow.

'Nope. When we talked earlier, I
spoke about you takin' 'em outa my
cells an' off into the hills.'

'Ah!'

'You gotta problem with that, Earl?'

'Er . . . no. No, Joe.'

'Good! Then, since it's gone midnight, let's git goin'.'

'Not jest yet. We'll wait till the last
light goes out.'

'That could be another hour or
more.'

'Unlikely; not on a Monday night.'

'I s'pose not. OK. We'll go back into
my office an' I'll brew us some coffee.'

'Fine.'

Stone waited until the four had
trooped back into the outer office and
the door had slammed shut behind

them. Thereupon, he pulled himself up so that he could peer inward and downward into the cells. This time he did spot the twins trussed up like a pair of Christmas turkeys. He dropped down again and stood for some moments thinking. Could he take on all four? Possibly. But could he do so without putting the youngsters' lives at risk? Unlikely. He needed reinforcements.

As this thought flashed through his mind, Stone observed a figure step out of the Trail's End saloon and begin to unhitch the piebald cayuse that was standing outside. The Kentuckian hurried across.

Upon arrival, he recognized the figure to be none other than the musician who had played the spoons at the Ace of Diamonds on the previous Saturday night.

'Can I have a word?' he asked.

The musician, having mounted the cayuse, peered down at the Kentuckian, who was standing illuminated by the light spilling out through the batwing doors.

'It's Mr Stone, ain't it?'

'That's right . . . er . . . ?'

'Everyone hereabouts calls me Two Spoons.'

'Wa'al, Two Spoons, I need your help.'

Two Spoons Farren looked most surprised. Since the shoot-out at the Ace of Diamonds, Jack Stone had become a celebrity in Boulder Creek. Tales of the famous Kentuckian gunfighter's prowess, some highly exaggerated, had spread through the town like wildfire. Two Spoons Farren was astonished, therefore, that such a man should require help from a mere musician.

'Sure . . . sure thing, Mr Stone. What . . . what can I do for you?' stammered Two Spoons Farren.

'You jest finished a stint at the Trail's End?'

'Yup.'

'So, I guess you're on your way home?'

'Yup.'

'Wa'al, I want you to delay your homecomin' an, instead, ride out to the Big Canyon with a message for Henry Turpin.'

'OK; I can do that. What's the message, Mr Stone?'

'Tell him that his nephew an' niece are bein' held here in town, in one of the cells at the back of the law office, an' that the sheriff is in cahoots with Earl Peplow.'

'I . . . I don't understand.'

'You don't have to, Two Spoons. Jest tell him to git here as soon as he can. I'll be waitin' at the rear of the law office.'

'But — '

'I dunno what you earn each week as a musician, but you deliver my message an' I'll guarantee Mr Turpin will reward you with a darned sight more'n you can earn in a month.'

Two Spoons Farren's eyes lit up.

'I'll do it!' declared the musician.

'As quick as you can,' said Stone.

The Kentuckian watched as the other galloped off northward along Main Street and quickly vanished into the darkness. Then he headed for the doorway of the dry-goods store, which stood immediately opposite the rear exit of the law office. Once again, he settled down to wait.

It was there that Henry Turpin found him when a little over half an hour later, he rode into town accompanied by his foreman, Max Wayne, the young, red-headed cowboy, Buck Walters, and three other hands. The six dismounted and Henry Turpin addressed the Kentuckian.

'Buck tells me you reckon Earl Peplow murdered his cousin in order to inherit, an' that he wants Ben an' Laura dead 'cause they witnessed his crime. Are you sure 'bout all this, Mr Stone?'

'I am,' said Stone.

'You sent Two Spoons to tell me that Ben an' Laura are bein' held prisoner in the law office.'

'I did.'

'I find it hard to believe that Joe Brand's got hisself involved.'

'Money talks.'

'I guess. So, what do we do?'

'I figure it's best to jump 'em when they bring your nephew an' niece outa there. If 'n' we try to storm the place, they could spot us comin' an' use Ben an' Laura as hostages.'

'Wa'al, what's holdin' 'em up?' demanded the rancher.

'Earl Peplow wants to wait till the last light goes out.' Stone jerked his thumb towards the Ace of Diamonds. 'Once the lights go out there, I expect they'll make their move.'

'OK, so what do we do meantime?'

'I dunno whether they'll bring Ben an' Laura out the back or out the front. I guess we'd best cover both exits.'

'Right.'

'I suggest you let me an' Buck an' another of your hands take the front, while you, Max an' the other two take the rear.'

'OK. Let's do that.'

The party promptly split in two, Stone and his two comrades-in-arms making their way silently and circuitously to a point opposite the law office's front door. This time they had not long to wait. Two minutes later the lights in the Ace of Diamonds were doused.

Inside the law office, Sheriff Joe Brand threw back the remains of his coffee and said briskly, 'OK, we can go now an' git them youngsters. We'll take 'em out the back door.'

'But the hosses are out front!' exclaimed Earl Peplow.

'Wa'al, go bring 'em round the back,' snapped Brand.

Peplow turned to Jed Burke and Bill Hudson.

'OK, boys,' he said. 'You two go fetch the hosses while me an' the sheriff take the kids out the back way.'

The two homesteaders, eager to get the whole business over and done with, quickly crossed the office and stomped out onto the stoop. It was as they were unhitching the horses that the first shot rang out. There was no doubt in either man's mind that the shot was fired somewhere in the rear of the law office.

'What in tarnation . . . ?' began Jed Burke, hastily drawing his revolver.

'You're surrounded. Drop your guns!' cried Stone from the shadows opposite.

Jed Burke, however, had no intention of surrendering. He swiftly loosed off a shot in the general direction of the Kentuckian's voice. As he did so, his confederate also went for his gun.

This was a mistake. Burke's shot had passed a foot or more to Stone's left. The Kentuckian's response was lethal. He pumped two quick shots into Burke and two into Hudson.

Stone's first shot penetrated Burke's left eye and exploded out of the back of his skull in a cloud of blood, brains and splinters of bone. His second, which was in fact superfluous, struck the homesteader in the chest as he fell backwards into the dusty street.

Bill Hudson survived only a few moments longer than Burke, for Stone's third shot hit him in the belly, while the Kentuckian's fourth smashed through his ribcage and literally ripped his heart in two.

The two men had no sooner collapsed dead beside their tethered horses than Buck Walters and his fellow cowhand began running across the street towards the law office. They dashed into the outer office and, observing that the door leading to the cells lay open, hurried through to the rear. These quarters were empty, but immediately outside the back door stood Earl Peplow and Sheriff Joe Brand. Peplow clutched a bloody arm, while Brand clutched Laura Johnson.

'What . . . what's happened?' gasped Walters.

Facing the law office were Henry Turpin, Max Wayne and the other two hands. All four held guns aimed at Peplow and the sheriff, and standing with them was Ben Johnson.

'Things didn't go exactly to plan,' growled a disconsolate Henry Turpin.

This was true. When Peplow and Brand had emerged from the rear of the law office with the two youngsters, Turpin had yelled at the twins to run for it and had promptly opened fire. The .45 calibre slug had hit Peplow in the arm and knocked him flat on his back. As he fell, Peplow had lost his grip of Ben, who, although still bound at the wrists and gagged, had straight-away made a dash for freedom.

Laura had not been so lucky, however. Before she could move, Brand had grabbed her tightly by the arm and, swiftly drawing his revolver, rammed the barrel hard against her head.

Peplow turned to face the new-comers.

'Don't try nothin',' he warned them. 'If 'n' you do, Joe'll blow the girl's brains out.'

'That's right,' confirmed the grim-faced sheriff.

'You ain't gonna git away with this,'

said Turpin angrily.

Earl Peplow and Joe Brand were no less angry. Their aspirations of becoming rich men were irrevocably dashed. All they could hope for now was to escape justice by fleeing the country.

'You want your niece to live, you're gonna do exactly as we tell you,' said Peplow.

There followed a short period of silence while Henry Turpin digested Peplow's words.

'Go on,' he rasped.

'There's some hosses hitched out front. Fetch two of 'em,' said Peplow.

'Max, go git 'em.'

The foreman scowled.

'You sure 'bout this, boss?' he enquired.

'I'm sure,' said Turpin.

'OK.'

They waited while Max Wayne brought the horses round to the rear of the law office. Then, while Joe Brand mounted one of them, Earl Peplow held his Remington to the girl's head.

'Drop your guns on the ground,' said Peplow.

'You gotta be kiddin'. We ain't — ' began Turpin.

'Drop 'em or I shoot the girl,' declared Peplow.

The rancher glowered.

'OK, boys, do as he says,' he muttered.

'You too,' said the sheriff to the two cowhands who remained inside the law office.

When Buck Walters and his pal inside and the rest outside had laid down their arms, Joe Brand replaced his revolver in its holster and, bending down, quickly hoisted the girl into the saddle in front of him. Then, grasping the reins with one hand, he again drew the gun and jabbed its barrel hard against the girl's ribs.

In the meantime, a one-armed Earl Peplow had, with some difficulty, mounted the other horse. He clutched at his wound for a moment or two before taking up the reins. Although sorely tempted, neither Henry Turpin nor any of his men had attempted to retrieve their weapons from where they had dropped them.

'OK; we're gonna ride outa here an' I don't want none of you to follow us,' stated Peplow.

'What . . . what are you aimin' to do with Laura?' demanded Turpin.

'Providin' you an' your men make no attempt to pursue us, we'll release her once we cross the border into Canada,' said Peplow.

'Hell, that ain't — ' began the rancher.

'Shuddup! That's the deal,' snapped Peplow. 'You accept it?'

'I . . . I reckon,' replied Turpin, with obvious reluctance.

'Good!'

Earl Peplow smiled sourly. Then, turning his horse's head, he set off at a canter northwards. Joe Brand and his prisoner followed a few paces behind.

'What now?' asked Max Wayne.

'We . . . we stay put,' grunted Henry Turpin, bending to retrieve his revolver.

'You're gonna let 'em git away?'

'I don't see we got any other choice, Max,' retorted the rancher.

Thereupon, he set to removing the gag from Ben Johnson's mouth and untying the cords that bound the youngster's wrists.

Earl Peplow and the sheriff, meantime, had broken into a gallop. They rode beneath a bright, starlit sky, anxious to reach and cross into Canada at the earliest possible moment. Once there, they would be safely outside the jurisdiction of the United States.

They had progressed no further than a couple of miles, however, when, upon rounding a bend in the trail, they found themselves confronted by a lone horseman. Indeed, they were almost on top of him before Joe Brand recognized the rider as the Kentuckian gunfighter, Jack Stone.

'Holy cow! How in tarnation did you . . . ?'

Brand's question was never completed, for Stone did not hesitate. He took careful aim and fired. Once; twice; thrice.

The Kentuckian's first shot whistled past Laura's cheek and struck the sheriff in the right shoulder, toppling both him and the girl out of the saddle. Stone's second and third shots hit Earl Peplow in the chest.

He, likewise, was knocked clean out of the saddle and, as he attempted to clamber to his feet, a fourth shot blasted his brains out.

Stone dismounted, slipped his Frontier Model Colt back into its holster and helped Laura to her feet. He quickly removed the gag and her bonds.

'You OK?' he asked anxiously.

'Y . . . yes, Mr Stone. I'm not hurt.'

The girl threw herself into his arms and, sobbing her heart out, thanked him over and over again for rescuing her from her captors. Stone held her close and gave her a series of reassuring pats.

Then, once she had recovered a little, he helped Laura mount one of the horses.

'You'll be OK to ride back into town, will you?' he said.

'Are . . . aren't you comin' with me?' enquired Laura.

'I'll be along directly. Jest gotta li'l business here to finish first,' replied the Kentuckian.

'Oh, all right! I'll see you back in town,' said the girl.

Stone watched her disappear round the bend in the trail and then turned his attention to Sheriff Joe Brand. The lawman had by now staggered to his feet. He clasped his wounded right shoulder, the blood trickling through between his fingers, and glared malevolently at the Kentuckian.

'How'd you git here?' he demanded.

'When I saw how things were, I guessed you'd wanta make for the border. So, while you were back of the law office, I jest mounted up an' rode on ahead of you,' replied Stone.

'Goddamit, I knew you'd be trouble first time I slapped eyes on you!' snarled Brand.

'If I'm trouble, you're a goddam disgrace,' retorted Stone. 'You're s'posed to uphold the law, not flout it.'

'Yeah. Wa'al, what are you gonna do, huh? Take me in? I guess I'll git me a prison sentence. But, considerin' that I've served the folks of Miller County pretty darned well over the years an' that my brother-in-law is now mayor of Boulder Creek, I reckon, if I claim to be downright sorry for what I've done an' plead for leniency, I'll git it.'

'It'll be more'n you deserve. You oughta swing.'

'So say you. But you won't be on the jury.'

'Guess not.'

'So, take me in.' Brand grinned maliciously and sneered, 'Since I ain't killed nobody, they won't hang me. Real sorry to disappoint you, Stone.'

'I'll bet you are!'

Brand laughed.

''Course you could jest gun me down. I know you'd like to. Only you ain't the kinda feller would shoot someone in cold blood.'

'You're right. I wouldn't shoot someone in cold blood,' said the Kentuckian. 'But then you've riled me so much, my blood's hotter'n the Arizona desert on the fourth of July!'

So saying, Jack Stone again drew his Frontier Model Colt and, smiling grimly, promptly shot the sheriff dead. Then he remounted the gelding and rode off, not towards Boulder Creek, but northwards in the direction of Great Falls and his friends' horse ranch.

## THE END

We do hope that you have enjoyed reading this large print book.

Did you know that all of our titles are available for purchase?

We publish a wide range of high quality large print books including:
**Romances, Mysteries, Classics**
**General Fiction**
**Non Fiction and Westerns**

Special interest titles available in large print are:
**The Little Oxford Dictionary**
**Music Book, Song Book**
**Hymn Book, Service Book**

Also available from us courtesy of Oxford University Press:
**Young Readers' Dictionary**
**(large print edition)**
**Young Readers' Thesaurus**
**(large print edition)**

For further information or a free brochure, please contact us at:
**Ulverscroft Large Print Books Ltd.,**
**The Green, Bradgate Road, Anstey,**
**Leicester, LE7 7FU, England.**
**Tel:** (00 44) 0116 236 4325
**Fax:** (00 44) 0116 234 0205

*Other titles in the*
*Linford Western Library:*

# A TOWN CALLED
# TROUBLESOME

## John Dyson

Matt Matthews had carved his ranch out of the wild Wyoming frontier. But he had his troubles. The big blow of '86 was catastrophic, with dead beeves littering the plains, and the oncoming winter presaged worse. On top of this, a gang of desperadoes had moved into the Snake River valley, killing, raping and rustling. All Matt can do is to take on the killers single-handed. But will he escape the hail of lead?